AMAZON BESTSELLING AUTHOR

L. A. CASEY

Bronagh
a slater brothers novella
Copyright © 2015 by L.A. Casey
Published by L.A. Casey
www.lacaseyauthor.com

Cover Design by Mayhem Cover Creations | Editing by Gypsy Heart Editing
Formatting by JT Formatting

This book is licensed for your personal enjoyment only. This book may not be re-sold or given away to other people. If you would like to share this book with another person, please purchase an additional copy for each recipient. If you're reading this book and did not purchase it, or it wasn't purchased for your use only, then please return to your favorite book retailer and purchase your own copy. Thank you for respecting the hard work of this author.
All rights reserved.
Except as permitted under S.I. No. 337/2011 – European Communities (Electronic Communications Networks and Services) (Universal Service and Users' Rights) Regulations 2011, no part of this publication may be reproduced, distributed, or transmitted in any form or by any means, or stored in a database or retrieval system, without prior written permission of the author. The scanning, uploading, and distribution of this book via the Internet or via other means without the permission of the publisher is illegal and punishable by law. Please purchase only authorized electronic editions and do not participate in or encourage electronic piracy of copyrighted materials. This is a work of fiction. Names, characters, places, brands, media, and incidents are either the product of the author's imagination or are used fictitiously. The author acknowledges the trademarked status and trademark owners of various products referenced in this work of fiction, which have been used without permission. The publication/use of these trademarks is not authorized, associated with, or sponsored by the trademark owners.

Bronagh / L.A. Casey – 1st ed.
ISBN-13: 978-1500850395 | ISBN-10: 150085039X

Dedication

To all the lasses on my street team who have supported me,
and continue to support me every day.
I love all your faces!

Chapter One	1
Chapter Two	13
Chapter Three	19
Chapter Four	35
Chapter Five	48
Chapter Six	58
Chapter Seven	66
Chapter Eight	74
Chapter Nine	82
Chapter Ten	98
ALEC – Chapter One	106
About the Author	124
Other Titles	125

Chapter One

"**H**appy birthday!"
I heard my sister's voice and I wanted to answer her, I really did. But I was too tired to even open my mouth.

"Bee? Hello? You're twenty-one today, get your lazy arse up!"

I grunted in response and remained still.

"Okay, I wanted to do this the easy way, but since you won't get up you have left me no choice..."

I heard her leave the room in defeat and I smiled to myself as I snuggled deeper into my pillow and tangled myself up in my duvet cover. I was so comfortable and content, but that contentment ended a few minutes later when my sister came back into my bedroom armed with a weapon.

A *deadly* weapon.

"Rise and shine!" Branna shouted.

For a split-second, things were quiet and normal, and then all of a sudden everything was freezing and wet. I screamed in shock and coughed when I breathed down water instead of oxygen. I panicked and kicked off my covers then scrambled up until I was standing in the middle of my bed. I screamed as the pain of the ice-cold water I was covered in touched every last one of my nerve endings...

"Branna!" I screamed in anger.

"I told you to get up, but you wouldn't listen."

I screamed again and wiped the water out of my eyes. I opened my eyes in time to see the back of Branna as she legged it out of my bedroom at top speed.

"I'm goin' to fuckin' kill you!"

With a roar, I jumped off my bed and almost broke my neck on the wet floor that I *wouldn't* be cleaning up. Once I steadied myself, I carefully walked out of my room until I was safe on the dry landing, where I wiped my feet on the carpet. I then took off like a bat out of Hell down the stairs in search for my so-called sister. I checked the sitting room first, but it was empty. I went back out into the hallway and glared at the closed kitchen door. I advanced and swung the door open when I was close enough to do so.

"Happy birthday!"

I ignored the cheers from the men who filled my kitchen and searched around their bodies for my victim.

"Damn, bumble bee, ever heard of pyjama pants?" Kane's husky voice asked.

Kane Slater was the brother of my boyfriend, Dominic Slater. Dominic had three older brothers—Ryder, Alec, and Kane. He also had a younger brother by three minutes. Yep, an identical twin by the name of Damien Slater.

The Slater brothers were five hot-headed, mouth-watering studs, and little ole me got to call one of them her fella.

I looked at Kane when he spoke and I raised my eyebrows when I noticed that his eyes were cast downwards on my body. I frowned and looked at Alec and Ryder, whose eyes were locked on the lower half of my body as well.

When my eyes landed on my boyfriend Dominic, I rolled my eyes because the muppet was chewing on his lower lip as he looked at my body like he wanted to eat me up.

I looked down at myself and realised that I was in my knickers. My very wet—and not in a sexy way—knickers. No pyjama trousers to be seen anywhere in sight.

Was I embarrassed?

No.

Was I angry?

Hell fucking yes!

"Branna," I growled.

Each of the brothers smiled at me then looked over their shoulders to where a crouching Branna was hiding... or trying to hide.

"You traitorous bastards!" she shouted then screamed bloody murder when I made a run for her.

She scrambled forward and maneuvered around Kane, who was now rubbing his chest and lightly coughing. The poor lad hasn't been feeling well lately. I would have stopped and checked if he was okay, but I was on a mission. I ignored him and the shouts from the other brothers for me to 'leave Branna alone' and focused on my sister who escaped out of the kitchen door and into the back garden.

"Leave me alone. I was only doin' what Dominic told me to do!" Branna shouted as she heaved herself up onto the large trampoline Dominic won in a Facebook competition last year.

I didn't know why he entered the competition. I honestly thought the trampoline would go to waste, but you would be surprised how often the brothers jump around on it like a bunch of children.

"I didn't tell you to pour water over her, you lying little—"

"Finish that sentence, Dominic. I dare you," Ryder's growling voice cut Dominic off.

I pulled my wet bobbin from my hair and then tied my hair back up into a messy bun. I laughed at Dominic, who looked like he wanted to stand up to Ryder, but knew better than to do so. Dominic could probably lay Ryder out, but then again, I've never seen Ryder fight, so for all I know he could destroy Dominic.

"I think what he was goin' to call her was a lyin', little STD carryin' slut... Which would be highly accurate."

Is that too harsh?

Dominic gasped. "I was only going to call her a bitch, not all of what you just said!"

Ryder punched Dominic in the shoulder and it made him hiss in pain. I found it funny. I turned back to the trampoline where my sister was jumping around like a child on a sugar rush.

"Stay away from me, Bronagh," she said, and from what I could see, the bitch was smiling.

She thinks she's funny?

We would see about that.

"You think this is funny? You think pourin' water over me is funny?" I snapped as I climbed up onto the trampoline.

"What I'm laughin' at is you chasin' me around in a wet tank top and a pair of knickers... wet *granny* knickers at that, they look awful."

I pulled back as if she slapped me. "You take that back! They are comfortable... I can't sleep in a thong or other shite like that, they split me in half!"

Branna devilishly smiled. "What does Dominic think of your granny knickers?"

I narrowed my eyes and shouted, "Dominic, do you care that I wear granny knickers to bed?"

"What? Um, no. I mean, I'd prefer if you wore nothing or at the very least a thong, but they all slide off the same way so I'm not bothered by them."

I heard Alec burst into laughter while I shook my head in disappointment—Dominic never failed to say the wrong thing.

"He doesn't care."

Branna smiled. "So, I heard."

I narrowed my eyes. "Come here."

"No."

I smiled. "Why?"

"Do you think I'm stupid?"

"Yes."

Branna ignored me and said, "I'm not goin' near you because I know you're gonna hit me when I get close enough."

I steadied myself on the moving trampoline. "You poured ice water over me head and destroyed me bed! I think a slap is a small price to pay for that horrible wake-up call."

"Your slaps hurt, though."

I raised my eyebrow. "All slaps hurt."

Branna shook her head. "You hit like a man, so your slaps hurt more."

I was offended, but also strangely pleased that she called me strong.

"Branna, you're a thirty-one-year-old woman. Start actin' your age."

Branna choked on air. "You're twenty-one today, and yet you're chasin' me around the house like a ten-year-old. You should look in the mirror before you tell people to act their age."

I snorted. "Whatever, nine more years and you're forty."

Ever since Branna turned thirty, no one was allowed mention the number forty, which, of course, meant I teased her that the forties train was coming for her all the time.

Branna screeched and came at me like a bull but because she was on the trampoline, she fell flat at my feet before she could put her hands on me. I heard the brothers' laugh when she fell and it made me chuckle, too. That was until Branna wrapped her hands around my ankles and pulled. I went flying up into the air until I came down and landed on my back with a bounce—literally.

"Oh, my God. That was brilliant! Dominic, did you *see* that?" I shouted with laughter.

"Yeah, I saw it, baby... and I can also see Branna crawling over to you."

"Bro, you ruined the element of surprise!" Alec snapped to Dominic making him laugh.

I stopped laughing and lifted my head up from the trampoline in time to see Branna pounce on me.

"No mercy!" I roared and rolled out of the way.

Branna face-planted into the trampoline, and while she was momentarily unmoving, I dove on her and pinned her hands behind her back while I sat on her arse to hold the rest of her body down.

"Get off me!" Branna snapped.

I raised my eyebrow and leaned forward, placing my mouth by her ear. "What part of no mercy don't you understand?"

"The whole concept! Let me up!"

I stayed put. "Apologise for throwin' water on me and I will."

Branna screamed in frustration.

"I'm not movin' till you say sorry."

Branna took in a few deep breaths and angrily said, "I'm sorry, okay?"

I had contemplated her apology for a moment before I got off her. Branna groaned and carefully got to her feet on the bouncy trampoline. She reached around and touched her arse then growled in my direction.

"I'm all wet because of you."

Served her right.

"Boo-hoo, I'm all wet. You dirty bitch."

Branna and I looked at Alec when he spoke in a bad imitation of Branna and we simply shook our heads at his nasty arse.

"You're disgustin'," I said to him.

He smiled and said, "I know."

I snickered and looked back at Branna when she unsteadily walked in my direction. I thought she was going to hit me so I blocked my face with my hands, but instead of punches, I felt her arms come around me.

"Happy birthday, baby," she murmured.

I opened my eyes and smiled as I put my arms around her and hugged her tightly back.

"Thanks, Bran."

I thought she was going to let me go, but she suddenly looped her leg behind mine and pushed me back by my shoulders. I slammed down onto the trampoline and it knocked the breath out of me.

"What was that for?" I wheezed.

"For pinnin' me," Branna said then began to jump up and down.

"Stop!" I groaned as I rolled from side to side on the trampoline.

I opened my eyes and watched Branna get off the trampoline with Ryder's assistance. I lifted my hand and gave her the finger when she looked back at me to which she laughed. She then pulled Ryder and Alec into the house while Dominic climbed up on the trampoline. He closed the netting of the trampoline and crawled over to me, rolled me onto my back and wiggled his way between my legs to hover over me.

"Can I help you?" I asked him, amused.

Dominic smiled. "Yeah, you can give me a kiss. I haven't had one since last night."

I shook my head. "I haven't brushed me teeth yet."

"So?"

"So, me breath smells like arse."

Dominic chuckled. "No, it doesn't."

He leaned his head down to mine and puckered his lips. I chuckled and quickly pressed my lips to his, but only for a second.

"That was a poor attempt, try again."

I groaned. "I'll kiss the lips off you *after* I brush me teeth... and shower."

Dominic grinned. "I could use a shower."

I deadpanned. "You showered this mornin' after you came back from your run, I heard you."

Dominic rubbed his nose against mine. "Do you know what time that was at?"

I shrugged. "Stupid o'clock?"

Dominic snickered. "Five thirty."

Like I said, stupid o'clock.

I scrunched up my face in horror. "There is somethin' wrong

with you. That is too early to do anythin' but sleep."

"I always wake up early, you know that."

I rolled my eyes. "Yeah I do, because you always touch me arse before you get out of bed and it wakes me up."

Dominic frowned. "I have to say goodbye to my baby and reassure her that I'll be back."

I forced myself not to smile.

"Stop referring to me arse as a separate person, it creeps me out."

Dominic placed all his weight onto his left arm and used his right hand to cover my mouth. "Shhhh! She will hear you."

I licked Dominic's palm, which he found disgusting.

"That's gross."

I snorted and mimicked his voice and accent. "That's gross."

Dominic narrowed his eyes at me and in my accent said, "Omigod, that's fuckin' nasty that is."

I burst into a fit of laughter. "Okay, that was spot on."

Dominic beamed. "I've got your accent mastered."

I snorted. "Yeah? Well, I have *you* wrapped right around me little finger."

Dominic grunted. "Don't I know it."

I smiled up at him as he took a moment to stare down at me before he lowered his head to mine and claimed my mouth with his. He grabbed my hands and thrust my arms above my head while he forced his tongue into my mouth.

I moaned in delight as Dominic placed more of his weight on me. I *loved* feeling him all over me.

I opened my eyes when I felt a certain part of Dominic harden and stand at attention. I turned my head to the side to break our kiss.

"Don't even think about it! We're out in the back garden!" I hissed, breathless from our kiss.

Dominic leaned off me a little and smiled. "The net around the trampoline is black. It's hard for us to see out, so it will be hard for people to see in."

Is he thinking public sex?

"Dominic, you *can't* be serious!"

He only waggled his eyebrows at me before he released my arms. He then moved backwards and grabbed the band of my wet underwear. In one swift motion, he pulled them down my legs and off my body.

"Dominic!" I screeched and tried to close my legs, but that was impossible because he was back between them.

When closing my legs failed, I used my hands to cup my vagina to try and reclaim some modesty.

"Everything okay?" I heard Alec's voice shout from the back-door.

"No, Dominic is—"

"Trying to get some. Tell her whether or not you can see us."

I lifted one hand up and tried to whack Dominic, but he grabbed it before my hand could make contact with his face and repinned it above my head. He looked smug as fuck while he pinned my arm again.

"He closed the net. You can't see in, bee, the colour of the nets when it's closed makes it virtually impossible. It's matte black," Alec assured me.

Jesus, help me.

"I. Don't. Care. I want—"

"Music, turn on some music!" Dominic shouted over me, cutting me off.

"Okay, I'll get my Beats speaker."

What. The. Hell?

"Alec, don't bloody listen to 'em!" I shouted but got no reply.

I snapped my head in Dominic's direction and glared up at him.

"I'm not messin' with you, let me up or I swear to God almighty that I will castrate you!"

Dominic laughed. "You need my balls for future babies—the last thing you would do is cut them off."

The thought of babies made me happy, but I kept a scowl on my face.

"You sure about that?" I snarled.

Dominic hesitated for a moment before he nodded. "Yes. Yeah. Yep. Very sure."

I am going to kill him.

"You're makin' me so bloody mad, I can feel myself wantin' to hurt you."

Dominic beamed down at me. "It's a good thing I have your good arm pinned then, right?"

I bucked under him, trying to use my pelvis as a weapon, but to no avail.

"What exactly are you doing?"

I closed my eyes and in a tearful tone said, "I just want to get up and go take a shower. I'm cold and wet."

Dominic didn't say anything, after twenty seconds or so, I opened my eyes and found him smiling down at me.

"I know the difference between when you're really upset and when you're just complaining, pretty girl. You aren't sad, you're just mad that I won't do what you want me to do."

I lifted my only remaining free hand up from my vagina and took a swing at Dominic that he caught. Again.

"You know something? I'm disappointed at how often you take a swing at me and miss. I either catch them all or you flat-out miss. You should be on point with on your throws. Honestly, babe, have your learned nothing from dating me?"

I narrowed my eyes to slits. "I learned that the male species are a bunch of bas—"

"Don't be dragging my fellow man down because you're in a mood with me."

I didn't know what to say back to him that didn't involve a million threats and curse words, so I simply closed my mouth and looked to my left, away from him and his stupidity.

"Wait a second... are you... are you not talking to me?" Dominic asked.

He didn't need to sound so fucking surprised.

"You *really* aren't talking to me?" Dominic asked.

I remained silent with my head turned away from him.

"Bronagh?" Dominic laughed.

I'm not fucking speaking to you right now!

"I love you, my pretty girl," Dominic murmured and that only annoyed me further because he was trying to use love to guilt me into speaking to him.

He could forget it! I was not speaking to him for at least ten hours.

"Happy birthday to you," he softly sang.

Oh, my God.

"Happy birthday to you."

Oh, my God, stop it.

"Happy birthday, my dear pretty girl."

Oh, my God, no.

"Happy birthday to you."

That wasn't fair.

I slowly turned my head until I was staring up at Dominic.

"You're a crap singer," I murmured.

Dominic smiled. "You broke your vow of silence."

I raised my eyebrows. "How did you know that I took a vow?"

"You vow a lot of things when you're mad," he laughed.

I turned my head as a smile curved my mouth.

"Ah-ha, I am forgiven."

I smiled wide as I shook my head and turned back to look at Dominic. "Thank you for singin' to me, that was so sweet."

Dominic smiled and leaned his head down to mine.

"I love you," he said.

I brushed my nose against his. "I love you, too, babe."

Dominic opened his mouth to say something but glanced up and smiled instead.

"Okay, I'm leaving my Beats speakers out here so don't forget to bring them inside in case it starts to rain. We're all going out, too, so don't worry about us coming back out here. Have fun."

Alec fucking Slater!

I wanted to curse at him, but he wouldn't have heard me even if I did because the tune "Birthday Sex" by Jeremiah blared throughout the back garden.

"Nice song choice," I growled cursing Alec in my mind.

Dominic smiled as he covered my mouth with his and pressed his weight down on me. He released my hands and dropped down to his elbows so he wouldn't be squishing me. I ran my hands up his arms over his shoulders and down his back.

"Off," I murmured into Dominic's mouth.

He sat back on his heels, grabbed the hem of his t-shirt and pulled it up over his head. As usual the sight of his bare chest and stomach sent me reeling.

He was a portrait of perfection.

"Fuck me," I breathed.

Dominic growled, "I intend to."

Chapter Two

Dominic leaned back down and retook his position of hovering over me.

I moved my hands over his bare back, feeling every ridge and muscle before I moved around to his stomach.

"I fuckin' love your abs and V line—they are so sexy."

Dominic lowered his head until his mouth was directly over my now hard nipple.

"I can see through your shirt," he murmured.

"Thanks to Branna soakin' me with water."

I felt my eyes flutter shut when Dominic's hot mouth closed over my nipple. I bit down onto my lower lip when the heat of his tongue swirled around my areola.

"Dominic," I whispered.

He hummed around my nipple before releasing it with a pop. He moved his head up to mine and claimed my mouth with his. He had kissed me hard and thoroughly before he put a hand under my neck. He pulled me up into a sitting position, and I momentarily wondered what he was doing until he broke our kiss and pulled my tank top over my head.

I gasped and involuntarily shivered as a cool breeze surrounded me. Dominic gently pushed me back down onto my back. Covering my body with his, he kept the cold at bay.

I could feel my clit spring to life with pulses of need, and just as I reached down to touch it, Dominic grabbed my hand.

"Mine," he growled.

I swallowed.

God, he is so hot.

"I need—"

"I know what you need, pretty girl, but *I'll* be the one to give it to you."

I looked up at the blue sky as Dominic disappeared. I lifted my head and looked down just as Dominic spread me with his fingers and flicked his tongue over my sensitive clit.

"Omigod," I groaned.

I couldn't help but look around as Dominic licked and sucked at me. I was convinced we could be seen and I hated that I found it so exciting.

"Birthday sex, birthday sex."

I groaned as the chorus of "Birthday Sex" filled the back garden. I rolled my hips, pushing my pelvis into Dominic's face to the beat of the song. He growled and carefully grazed his teeth over my clit, causing my lower body to twitch.

With his face buried between my legs, he used his left hand to grab onto the flesh of my hip to hold me down. He moved his right hand to my entrance where he lightly drew circles around the outside of my entrance, teasing me.

It tickled and gave me shivers.

"Oh, please," I groaned, making sure to keep my voice low.

Dominic hummed and slipped one finger inside me, then two.

Yes.

He rotated his fingers as he pumped them in and out of me, the rhythm of his finger's movement along with his tongue swirling around my clit started to become a little much.

My breath quickened and my heart rate picked up as I broke out in a sweat.

"Dominic, I'm close."

He used the hand on my hip to reach up and caress my breast, the action caused my back to arch. I licked my dry lips and clenched my hands into fists since I had nothing to grab.

"Ahhh," I groaned.

I felt my inner muscles begin to clench around Dominic's fingers. The familiar feeling was always my warning that my body was about to experience ecstasy.

"Yes!" I gasped when Dominic suddenly curved his fingers and stroked my g-spot, rubbing it violently while he bore down on my clit and sucked harder.

My body exploded.

My hips bucked against Dominic's face as my eyes rolled back, my back arched, my breathing halted, and every nerve ending I had was alive and burning.

When I found my breath again and managed to open my eyes, Dominic's face was there.

Smirking.

"First birthday present, delivered."

I'm sorry, what?

"I don't know what you're talkin' about, but I honestly don't care."

Dominic snickered then leaned down and kissed my nose.

"How do you feel?"

I lazily smiled. "Satisfied."

Dominic winked. "You ain't seen nothing yet, baby."

I raised my eyebrows as I spread my legs a little wider.

"I'm ready."

Dominic gripped my thighs. "I know you are, dirty girl, but penetration is the last present of the day."

Hold the fuck on.

"You mean to tell me you *aren't* goin' to fuck me? What is wrong with you? Are you ill? Is it serious?"

Dominic looked down at me, his features scrunched together.

Oh, Christ.

It is serious!

"Bronagh, I'm fine."

Lies.

"No, you aren't. Sex always comes after oral. It always has... Somethin' is wrong if—"

"Nothing is wrong," Dominic laughed. "I've got a list that I'm sticking to that's all."

A list? What?

"I'm so confused."

Dominic waggled his eyebrows. "Perfect. Let's go."

I didn't move an inch.

"I'm naked... you threw me clothes behind you. Get me them first."

Dominic sighed and reached for his t-shirt. He held it out to me then dropped it on my chest as he unsteadily got to his feet.

"That t-shirt is long enough for you to run back inside the house without showing your phat ass to the world."

Dick.

I grumbled as I pulled the plain white t-shirt over my head, which was a little difficult to do with Dominic jumping up and down, though.

"Stop it!"

He didn't stop.

"We have *got* to fuck in here. The bouncing would be perfect for when you're on top. Why haven't I thought of it before?"

I had a few ideas.

"Because your little mind—"

"Shut it, Murphy. I'm not listening to your insults today. I've got a plan, and insults are not on my list."

A plan and a list?

"Are you high?" I asked as I carefully got to my feet.

Dominic looked at me and his expression was lost.

"I don't take drugs... you know that."

I laughed. "I know, but you're bein' weird, so I had to ask."

Dominic jumped over to the trampoline exit and slid through the net. I followed him and went out headfirst so he could grab under my armpits and lift me down. I gripped onto the hem of Dominic's t-shirt as he did this so no one saw my arse.

"So, what is this list and plan you're talkin' about?" I asked as I picked up Alec's Beats speakers and walked ahead of Dominic back into our house.

Yes, *our* house.

Dominic and I lived in my house now while Branna lived with Ryder, Kane, and Alec at their house in Upton. It was only on a trial basis to see if we could handle living with each other. It'd been two months since Dominic moved in and Branna moved out, and no one had died or been severely injured.

So far, so good.

"It's your birthday and I have planned out the entire day for you."

I turned to Dominic when he slid the back door closed.

"You did?"

Dominic nodded. "I wanted to do something special for you since you mean so much to me."

Oh, my goodness.

"Dominic," I whispered as my eyes welled up with tears.

His eyes widened as he shot to my side. "Don't cry, no tears are allowed on your birthday."

I laughed and cried as I wrapped my arms around his waist.

"I can't *not* cry when you say and do somethin' so romantic."

Dominic rested his head on mine and put his arms around me.

"Alec can go fuck himself—he said I couldn't be romantic. Proved him wrong."

I laughed and kissed Dominic's still bare chest.

"I love you."

Dominic leaned down and kissed my forehead. "I love you, too, very much, my pretty girl."

I smiled then yelped when a stinging slap was delivered to my arse.

"Go get showered. I have a schedule to follow."

I grumbled as I rubbed my bum and walked away from him. I paused mid-stride and glanced over my shoulder.

He smirked at me. "Go on, get."

Damn, he is serious.

I turned, and with a sudden burst of energy, I ran down the hall and up the stairs feeling more than eager to get showered and dressed.

I couldn't wait to see what Dominic had planned for me.

Chapter Three

"Indoor rock climbin'? You thought *indoor rock climbin'* would be a romantic thing we could do on me birthday? I *hate* physical exercise Dominic, you might as well have brought me to the bloody gym!"

The two men who were behind the reception desk of Gravity Climbing Centre averted their gazes but had smiles on their faces.

Dominic placed his hands on my shoulders. "I know you aren't a huge fan of exercise—"

He paused when he saw the look of disgust on my face.

"Okay, I know you aren't a fan of exercising *at all*, but it's not just wall climbing... Your second present is at the top of your climb."

I groaned. "You're makin' me work for it?"

Dominic pumped his eyebrows. "Oh, yeah, baby."

The men chuckled but coughed to cover it up when I shot them a dirty look. I narrowed my eyes then switched my gaze back to Dominic.

I couldn't be angry at him. He was doing something he thought was nice for me, so I would stow the bitchiness and be grateful, for now.

"Okay. I'm game, babe. Which wall do we have to climb?" I asked.

Dominic looked at the two men who then both checked the computer screen and grinned.

"Terrorised."

I froze. "Why the hell would you name a climbin' wall somethin' so bloody scary?"

Dominic face palmed himself while both men shrugged their shoulders at me. I knew I was being rude, but fucking hell, it was basically called the wall of terror.

"Where is this wall?" I asked.

Both men pointed behind me, and after taking a deep breath, I turned around and felt my jaw drop. I had to tilt my head back just to see the top of the wall.

"Dominic, you *can't* be fuckin' serious."

Dominic and both men laughed.

"It's a beginner's wall."

It is huge.

"I don't wanna see the advanced walls if this is a fuckin' beginner wall."

I'm going to die.

"I won't live to see this day through," I murmured.

Dominic swung his arm over my shoulder.

"You'll be fine. I'll be right behind you and your phat ass."

That didn't give me much comfort.

I numbly followed Dominic over to the terrifying wall and stared mutely at a small, fit looking woman who gave us instructions and tips.

I knew I was fucked with this activity because I couldn't remember a single word she had said after she finished speaking.

Not. A. Single. Word.

I swallowed when she bent down and picked up some harnesses. She handed a black one to Dominic and held onto a pink one that I assumed was for me.

"I'll help you get this harness on, Bronagh, since you're a beginner."

I nodded my head to the woman and placed my hands on her shoulders as she bent down and helped get my legs into the correct leg holes.

"I'll make the grip around your hips a little looser, the current fit will be a little tight."

I snapped my eyes to Dominic when he snorted and used his hands to make the shape of my arse.

Muppet.

The woman shimmied the harness up my body and tightened it around my waist. I licked my lips as she grabbed a little bag filled with white powder and strapped it around my hips.

The woman smiled at me then turned me to Dominic, who had a black helmet in his hand, he stepped forward and placed it on my head and clipped the strap under my chin. He leaned down and kissed my lips.

"You're going to be fine."

I'm not.

"Why do I feel like I'm doin' somethin' very wrong then?"

Dominic laughed. "Because you're just scared."

I blew out a large breath and turned to the wall. "Where is the thing that clips onto the harness so if I fall I don't die a horrible and painful death?"

"Sarah is getting that ready for you."

I looked and smiled at the woman who helped me get the harness on. I clearly missed that her name was Sarah, but I felt a little better now that I knew it.

I turned back to Dominic and frowned. He was wearing the same things as I was, only his harness had no silver clip and he had no helmet on.

"Where does your rope clip onto and where is your helmet?" I asked.

"I'm free climbing."

He said that like I knew what it meant.

"What does that mean?"

"I free climb the walls without equipment."

For real?

"You not goin' onto that death trap without a safety rope and helmet!"

Dominic bit down on his bottom lip so he wouldn't laugh.

"I'm not jokin', Dominic. It's dangerous!"

I turned to Sarah. "Tell him he needs his safety equipment."

Sarah chuckled. "Dominic is a regular here, he free climbs all the time."

He does?

I turned back to Dominic. "You do?"

He laughed at me. "Where do you think I go when I say I'm going climbing?"

I honestly had no idea. I never really paid much attention to him when he had his gym bag and workout clothes on. I always figured he was going to work out with one of his clients.

"I don't know," I murmured.

Dominic reached for me and pulled me into him. "It's going to be okay."

I took in a breath then said, "It better be a good bloody present."

Dominic snickered.

"Ready?"

No.

"Yeah."

Dominic turned me around, slapped my behind, and nudged me closer to Sarah. Sarah stepped forward and hooked the safety rope onto my harness.

"How are you feelin'?" she asked.

"Like I'm goin' to get sick."

Sarah nodded her head. "That's just your adrenaline startin' to kick in. You will be perfectly safe. Your belay device, that's this right here," she said as she tapped on the silver clip on my harness, "will work as a brake on your rope if you fall. It also clips onto the rope I have down here, so if you need to come down at any point, just shout down to let me know, and I'll lower you down to the ground, okay?"

No.

"Okay."

"Great, now get some chalk on your hands. It makes gripping onto the jugs easier."

I had no idea what she was talking about. I wished I hadn't zoned out when she was telling us what to do earlier.

Sarah moved off to the right and Dominic suddenly appeared in front of me. He reached for the little bag on my hips and dipped his fingers inside. His now white fingers covered my hands as he rubbed the chalk all over them.

"I wish I could fuck you right now," Dominic murmured.

I looked up at him wondering what the hell was wrong with him.

"I'm worried I might die and you're thinkin' of shaggin'?"

Dominic smirked. "It's seeing you in the harness, it makes my dick hard."

He was easily turned on.

"I bet me arse looks huge in it."

"Your ass *is* huge."

Dickhead.

"Okay," I breathed. "Let's get this over with."

Dominic kissed me quickly before he moved aside and gestured to the wall. "Ladies first."

What a fucking moment for him to be chivalrous!

I hesitantly stepped forward to the wall. I tilted my head all the way back and looked up.

It was high, but not *that* high.

I can do this.

I placed my hands on the things that stuck out of the wall. I couldn't remember what Sarah called them, but they were holders to me so that was what I decided to call them.

"Don't tense so much. You will slip."

I glanced over my shoulder and got a fright; I wasn't expecting Dominic to be right there.

"Relax, baby, you will be fine."

If he said that one more time, I was going to smack him.

"Back up, I've got this."

Dominic held his hands up and took a few steps back.

I turned back to the wall and focused. I gripped onto the holders and tried not to tense up so much. I placed my feet onto the smaller holders below me to keep steady before I reached up to a holder above me. I caught it and pulled myself up then repositioned my feet.

I have this.

I spent a few minutes climbing and I thought I made good progress until I looked down.

I was only six foot and four inches from the ground, I knew that because that was Dominic's height and my feet were level with his head!

"Oh, my God! I thought I was higher up... I don't wanna do this anymore!"

I heard Dominic and Sarah laugh and that annoyed me.

"This isn't funny. I want to come down!"

"Hold your horses, you're doing great. Slow and steady does it, baby."

Slow and steady. Ha!

"You've never done slow and steady in your life!" I snapped.

Male laughter was all I heard.

"Not with you, baby."

I looked around and found there were other people climbing the wall, and like me, they had someone like Sarah holding a safety rope for them on the ground. But the people who were holding their safety ropes were looking up at me and they were laughing at what

Dominic said.

Oh, God.

"I'm gonna kill you," I growled and used my anger to climb.

My anger ran out after thirty seconds along with my energy.

"Oh, God, I really need to exercise," I wheezed as I reached for another holder.

I screamed when I slipped. I managed to grab onto my holder, I couldn't help but look down and notice I was higher up this time.

A lot higher up.

"Hang on," Dominic shouted.

What else would I do, let go?

"No fuckin' shit!" I bellowed.

I blocked out the laughter from people around me and focused on not letting go of the wall even though my arms and thighs screamed for me to do so.

I began to get a little teary then.

"Dominic. Help!" I called out.

Silence.

"Okay, I'm coming. Don't be scared."

I closed my eyes and tried to think of something else, but my mind wouldn't focus so I opened my eyes and looked down. I narrowed my eyes as Dominic jumped up and grabbed onto a holder and pulled himself up onto the wall. He then proceeded to climb up to me like a fucking spider monkey.

He reached me in ten seconds tops.

"Hey, pretty girl."

He was behind me now as he placed a hand on my back and stroked.

"You're doing really good, you're almost halfway there."

Almost halfway.

Almost.

"Who invented this?"

"What, rock climbing or indoor climbing?"

"Both."

"Why?"

"Because I want to know the name of the bastard who is goin' to be the reason I die today, so when I arrive at the pearly white gates I can put a complaint in against him."

Dominic laughed.

"How do you enjoy this?" I asked. "Me limbs are burnin'."

"I'm used to it, babe. I can climb the beginner walls in seconds."

I rolled my eyes.

"Now is not the time to show off, Dominic."

Dominic chuckled and pressed a kiss on my back.

"I'm right here with you. I won't let you fall."

I scoffed. "You don't have a safety rope, so I'm not trustin' you with me life right now... You're actually fucked if you fall because you're not havin' *my* rope, and I'm not brave enough to try and save you up here."

I yelped when he smacked my arse.

"Cut out the yapping and keep climbing."

Bossy bastard.

"Okay, okay," I breathed.

I looked up and reached for a holder but missed it. I didn't fall back, but I did get a little unsteady.

"Bend your knee and place your foot on the blue foot chip then push off from that and reach for the purple jug directly above you. You can hoist yourself up easily from that."

Foot chip?

Jug?

"I don't fuckin' know what you're talkin' about! What is a jug chip?"

Dominic burst into laughter, and it really wasn't helping me.

"Do you mean the holder things sticking out of the wall? I don't care what the real names are, I'm callin' them holders because I'm holdin' onto them for dear life."

I was pretty sure that Dominic pressed his face into my back because I felt his breath through my tank top.

"What are you doin'?" I asked.

"I want to kiss you so badly right now. I hate that you're being so cute and are out of my reach."

I needed to get off this bloody wall, and he wanted to kiss me.

His priorities were so messed up.

I blocked out Dominic's touch and bent my knee like he told me to. I placed my foot on a blue little holder then reached up and grabbed the big purple holder and pulled myself up.

"Good girl, keep moving."

I did just that.

My arms were tired and my legs hurt like crazy, but I kept climbing and after five or so minutes, I reached the top.

"I did it. Dominic, I'm at the top!" I squealed in delight.

Dominic climbed up on my right side and smiled as he leaned in and kissed me.

"Told you that you could do it."

I was pretty pleased with myself.

Dominic reached into his back pocket and took out his phone then pointed it at me.

"Smile."

I did as asked and smiled a big cheesy smile.

Dominic chuckled then flipped the camera on his screen and moved his head next to mine. He held his phone out in front of us and I automatically turned my head and kissed Dominic's right cheek dimple as he smiled.

He laughed then turned his head and kissed me, taking a picture of that, too. We took more of us just smiling before he put his phone away.

"Why so many pictures?" I asked.

He shrugged. "No reason."

I eyed him, but the thought of my present grabbed my attention and I looked around the top of the wall. I spotted a pink box sitting on top of a large holder so I climbed my way over to it, grabbed it, put it in my mouth, then side climbed back over to Dominic.

"I found it," I said around the box.

Dominic grinned. "You going to open it now or when we're on the ground?"

"Hold onto my harness so I don't fall and I'll do it now."

Dominic got a good hold of my holder—or jug as he would call it—with his right hand then with his left hand he held tightly onto my harness.

"I've got you."

I trusted him completely so I let go of the wall and with both hands I opened the pink box. I stared at the little black book that had 'Bronagh' engraved in purple over the front of it. I took the book out of the box and placed the box on a holder.

I examined the book and then opened it.

The wind was knocked out of me when I read the title page.

100 Reasons Why I Love You.

"Dominic," I said and instantly started crying.

Dominic chuckled and pulled me into him. "Stop crying, you big baby."

I sobbed as I turned the page and read every one of the reasons why he loved me.

1: I love you because your smile because makes my day better.
2: I love you because your laugh gives me butterflies.
(Yeah, guys get them, too.)
3: I love you because your personality is awesome.
4: I love you because you possess the sexiest,
phatest ass known to man.
5: I love you because you let me touch your ass in public and do filthy things to it in private.
6: I love you because you have sex with me.
7: I love you because you give me blowjobs without my having to ask for them.

8: I love you because you're up for anything sexually. (GODDESS!!)
9: I love you because you can cook.
10: I love you because you have a wonderful, caring nature.
11: I love you because you have brains. (My little Einstein.)
12: I love you because your humour is on point.
13: I love you because you have a temper. (Yeah, I love it.)
14: I love you because you get jealous. (It's hot.)
15: I love you because you're kind.
16: I love you because you're selfless.
17: I love you because you give me a blowjob every day when you're on your period so I don't get upset.
18: I love you because you're honest.
19: I love you because you're blunt.
20: I love you because you cuss like a sailor.
21: I love you because you love me.
22: I love you because you don't get mad when I play on my Xbox for hours at a time.
23: I love you because you love my family.
24: I love you because you make me laugh.
25: I love you because you stand by me no matter what.
26: I love you because you trust in me.
27: I love you because you hold onto me so tightly when we sleep.
28: I love you because you talk in your sleep and say the weirdest shit.
29: I love you because you don't know how stunningly beautiful you are.
30: I love you because you willingly want to date me.
31: I love you because you don't mind that I fight.
32: I love you because you like watching me train.
33: I love you because you will try anything once.
34: I love you because you love pizza as much as I do.
35: I love you because you always find a way to wow me.
36: I love you because your body is a wonderland.

37: I love you because you laugh at my jokes, even if they aren't funny.
38: I love you because have never wrecked my car. (Knock on wood.)
39: I love you because you clean the bathroom.
40: I love you because you know how to sort laundry.
41: I love you because you know how to iron.
42: I love you because you don't drink my beer.
43: I love you because you know me better than anyone, even Damien. (Don't tell him that.)
44: I love you because we love the same candy.
45: I love you because you always tell me goodnight.
46: I love you because you do the grocery shopping.
47: I love you because you give me morning sex.
48: I love you because you like sports.
49: I love you because you have a girl crush on Mila Kunis.
50: I love you because you said if we could ever have a threesome with Mila Kunis you would be game.
51: I love you because you cry so easily.
52: I love you because my cock is the only cock your pussy knows and will ever know.
53: I love you because you're my definition of perfection.
54: I love you because you always smell good.
55: I love you because you love scary movies.
56: I love you because you don't force me to watch chick flicks.
57: I love you because you let me cop a feel whenever I want.
58: I love you because you're random.
59: I love you because you're awkward.
60: I love you because you let me pull your hair. ;)
61: I love you because you squeeze the toothpaste from the bottom of the tube.
62: I love you because you have beautiful, big, green eyes.
63: I love you because you put up with my snoring.
64: I love you because you're my best friend.

(Again, don't tell Damien.)

65: I love you because you can make sarcastic comments while keeping a straight face.
66: I love you because you're my high school sweetheart.
67: I love you because you tell me that you love me every day.
68: I love you because you will house and give birth to my babies.
69: I love you because you let me use your hair dryer.
70: I love you because you love me in spite of my past.
71: I love you because you don't take things so seriously.
72: I love you because you love life.
73: I love you because you look me in the eyes when you talk to me.
74: I love you because you kiss me to shut me up.
75: I love you because you don't care what people think.
76: I love you because you give me breakfast in bed on my birthday followed by sex.
77: I love you because you NEVER say you're tired when I try to get some from you.
78: I love you because your sex drive is as high as mine.
79: I love you because you refuse to completely grow up.
80: I love you because you're an animal lover.
81: I love you because you inspire me.
82: I love you because you're my home.
83: I love you because you're sexy as hell.
84: I love you because you're wild.
85: I love you because you make my heart smile.
86: I love you because you rock my world.
87: I love you because you say sorry when you know you're in the wrong.
88: I love you because you put all your energy into messy fighting with me.
89: I love you because we agree to disagree.
90: I love you because you make me a better person.
91: I love you because you are my everything.
92: I love you because you own the name pretty girl.

93: I love you because you're sassy.
94: I love you because even when I'm mad, you still love me.
95: I love you because you think it's okay to smack me at any point during the day for any given reason, then apologise for it later.
96: I love you because I can.
97: I love you because I do.
98: I love you because I would NEVER spend three hours making a book of 100 reasons why I love you for anyone else but you.
99: I love you because you're simply you.
100: I love you far more than just these 100 reasons.
You are my everything, pretty girl. I *love* you.

P.S. DO NOT SHOW THIS TO MY BROTHERS

I was a mess—a crying, blubbering mess.

"I c-an't b-believe—"

"Baby, breathe." Dominic smiled.

He couldn't wipe my face because he had no free hands, and I couldn't wipe my face because I was too busy hugging my book to my chest.

"Sarah, she's coming down. Get ready."

"Ready."

Dominic slowly pushed me out away from the wall, and I began to slowly descend back to the ground. I twirled around as I was lowered to the ground; I was still crying and hugging my book to my chest.

I felt my feet touch the ground then a few seconds later his scent surrounded me as he put his arms around my body.

"Maybe I should have left the book till last."

I laughed and cried as I wrapped my arms around him.

"I-I l-love i-it."

I was crying hard.

Dominic hushed me and swayed me from side to side for a few minutes. When my sniffles slowed down, he pulled back and laughed.

"You're so attractive."

I shoved him and quickly took the tissue from Sarah's outstretched hand. I thanked her, then wiped my eyes and blew my nose. I took a deep breath and sniffled a little more.

"I love it so much. I love *you* so much."

Dominic kissed my head. "I love you, too."

I knew he did. I had the book of reasons to prove it.

"This is the best present I've ever received. Thank you."

Dominic pushed loose strands of hair out of my face.

"That was only your second present. I have a few more to give you."

I gasped. "Really?"

Dominic nodded.

"Can I have them now?"

"No," he laughed, "You will get them at each location."

Each location?

"How do you—"

"I have a list, remember?"

Ah, yes, his list.

"Okay, now that we're done wall climbin'... I mean we *are* done wall climbin', right?"

Dominic nodded his head.

Oh, thank God.

"Great, so where to next?" I asked excited to see what else he had in store for me.

Dominic helped me out of my harnesses then lightly tapped my behind.

"To get some food."

Oh.

"I'm in me gym clothes. I'm not dressed to go out for food."

Dominic winked. "I have a change of clothes for you in my car. Branna packed them for me when you were sleeping this morning."

Oh.

"Oh, okay. Where are we goin'?"
Dominic smirked. "Wait and see."

Chapter Four

"Why are we in Phoenix Park? Are you takin' me to the zoo?" I gasped.

Dominic snorted. "And listen to you complain about all the children in your way so you can't see the penguins? No thanks."

I scoffed. "That was one time—"

"It happens every time we go to the zoo."

I folded my arms across my chest. "They purposely stand in the way of adults. It annoys me."

Dominic shook his head as he laughed. "A lot of things annoy you."

"So?"

Dominic didn't reply, he only mumbled to himself as he led me somewhere in Phoenix Park by the hand. I followed him mutely but looked down to my bag when my phone rang. I reached into it with my free hand and answered the phone before I put it to my ear.

"Hello?"

"Happy birthday!"

I smiled. "Thanks, Gav."

Dominic's hand tightened its hold on mine, and it made me roll my eyes.

His childlike grudge against Gavin was still as strong as when we were eighteen and in school. It was a very painful headache to deal with.

"Where are you? I have a card and present to give you."

I smiled.

"Aww, thank you! You didn't have to get me anythin'."

Gavin chuckled. "I know, but I wanted to. It's your twenty-first after all!"

Every time someone said that, all I could think of was that I only had another nine years until I celebrated my thirtieth birthday... that was scary.

"Well, thank you. That is so sweet of you—Ow!"

I snatched my hand from Dominic's suddenly painful grasp and stormed ahead of him.

God, he pissed me off sometimes!

"What's wrong? Are you okay?"

"I'm fine."

"Okay, so can I drop your stuff by... or is Dominic around?"

I grinned. He was so wary of Dominic.

"I'm in Phoenix Park with him. He has a bunch of things planned for us today."

Gavin sighed. "I'll give my present to Aideen then, and she can give it to you later or give it to Branna to give to you."

Aideen Collins was Gavin's older and only sister. She was good friends with Branna and was funny and completely bat-shit crazy.

She fit right in with us.

"Thanks, Gav, why don't you swing by later? I'm sure we're all goin' out somewhere tonight."

"Thanks for the invite, but I'm at work until eleven. I'll be shite company from fallin' asleep standin' up."

I snorted. "Okay well, come by durin' the week so we can watch a film or somethin'."

"You're on. Speak soon, hun."

I grinned, he said hun like an old woman.

"Bye, *hun*," I replied.

He laughed and hung up.

I put my phone in my bag and felt *him* close behind me as I had done so.

"You hurt me hand, you know?"

Dominic sighed. "Sorry, I just hate—"

"You hate Gavin. I know that, he knows that, the whole fuckin' world knows that, Dominic."

Silence.

"I just hate that you're close with him."

I turned to Dominic and glared up at him.

"I warned you before not to start this argument up again, and yet, you've started it. If you can't handle that one of me best friends is a fella, then you might as well pack up your shite and move out of me house and life because he isn't goin' anywhere. He is me *friend*. I don't know how many times I have to tell you that."

Dominic narrowed his eyes back at me.

"And I warned you not to threaten me with breaking up. I'll end up killing someone over it, Bronagh, you fucking know how mad it gets me."

I did, but he got me mad with his constant hang-ups about Gavin.

"Then grow up and accept I have a male friend. Honestly, Dominic, are you worried that I'll cheat on you or somethin'?"

Dominic went red in the face. "No, it's not you, it's him. *He* likes you. He always has."

I threw my hands up in the air just to avoid wrapping them around his neck.

"That was *years* ago! *He* is the one who decided on us just bein' friends, you remember that night, right? You ruined me first date."

Dominic had the audacity to laugh. "Yeah, and you started dating me instead... I also fingered you for the first time in that hospital examination room. Good times."

Oh. My. God.

"You fuckin' infuriate me!" I snapped and shoved him in the chest before turning and storming away from him.

He jogged after me, though.

"Do you even know where you're going?"

I didn't.

Phoenix Park was huge, and I was in a part of it that I had never been in before.

"No, but I'll follow this path and get out eventually. Then I'll get a taxi home—away from fuckin' you, you stupid fuckface bastard."

I was mad, and when Dominic laughed at me when I was mad, I became murderous—and laughing at me was exactly what the cunt did.

I turned around and rushed at him with a screech.

He dodged my swinging hands, grabbed my shoulders, then crooked his leg behind my knee and pushed. I gasped when my back touched the ground.

That bastard tripped me up!

I tried to get up, but Dominic was on me within a second.

"Listen to me crazy, calm down or one of us is going to get arrested. We're out in public. We aren't at home where we can kill each other then fuck it out."

Fuck it out?

Bastard!

"I'm *never* going to have sex with you again. Do you wanna know why? Because I'm goin' to cut your fuckin' dick off when you are least expectin' it!"

Dominic gazed down at me with gleeful eyes.

"Every time you say you won't have sex with me, I get you on your back and fuck you so hard that you cry when you come. This challenge has been set and completed millions of times before, pretty girl, you might as well stop it."

I growled because that was true.

Very true.

"I hope me vagina closes up and never gives you access again."

Dominic shrugged. "Your asshole feels just as good wrapped around my cock. I won't be that sad."

Oh, my God!

"You're a bastard."

"You're a bitch."

Gah!

"It's not nice to call me a bitch."

Dominic raised an eyebrow then said, "You will get over it."

Prick.

I huffed and looked away from him. He took it as an invitation to kiss my cheek.

"Please calm down. I don't want today to be about arguing. Please just try and control your temper… just for today."

I frowned.

My behaviour bothers him?

"Since when do you want me to control me temper?"

Dominic shrugged. "Since we hit our twenties and your tantrums stopped being cute."

Well, excuse me.

"Tantrums are never cute."

Dominic smiled. "Stop throwing them then."

Dick.

I took a breath and exhaled.

"Can we get to your birthday picnic now? It's only around the next bend."

I gasped. "A picnic? We're goin' on a picnic?"

We've never gone on a picnic before!

"We are." Dominic smiled.

I leaned up and kissed him hard on the mouth, and as always, our argument with its name-calling and threats was forgotten... until the next time we fought.

Dominic stood up then helped me to my feet. We walked down the pathway and around the bend to where Ryder Slater stood over a beautifully laid out picnic.

"Uh... hey, Ry."

Ryder winked at me then turned and walked off without saying a single word.

I looked at Dominic.

"What was that?"

Dominic shrugged. "He set this up then stood guard until we came. He is going back home now."

I gasped. "He drove an hour from home just to come into the city to set up a picnic for us?"

"Yes."

"God, I love your brothers."

Dominic chuckled. "They love you, too."

I skipped over to the picnic and sat down. Dominic laughed and sat down across from me. He opened a huge basket and reached inside and I burst out laughing when he lifted out a bucket of KFC chicken pieces.

"What? You think I can survive this day on your sandwiches? Please."

I shook my head still laughing as he grabbed some paper plates, napkins, and plastic forks and placed them in front of us. I sat patiently as he poured chips onto my plate followed by chicken pieces and beans.

"That smells *so* good!"

Dominic looked up and gave me a knowing look.

"It's a one-time thing, okay?"

I rolled my eyes.

"I'm serious. Every time you eat fast food, you complain about gaining weight."

"Fat food," I mumbled.

"What?"

"It should just be called fat food not fast food. The person who added in the 's' was a clever little fucker."

Dominic snickered. "You've gone six weeks without stepping foot inside a McDonald's, Burger King, or even a KFC. You're doing awesome, and you've lost a dress size to show for it."

I stared at him. "How do you know I lost a dress size?"

Dominic shrugged. "You buy your clothes from ASOS on my debit card, and you use my account. I get an email with your order, and it tells me the sizes of the items you bought."

I mentally grumbled.

I was not smart with computers, emails, or debit cards. Whenever I needed them, I would just use Dominic's accounts for everything. I gave him the money, of course; I wasn't *that* type of girlfriend.

"I lost a size on top, not on the bottom."

Dominic grinned.

"It's not a good thing, me arse is—"

"Perfect the way it is," Dominic cut me off as he dished up his food. "You stress that you have a pear-shaped body and that you have a big ass because you have big hips. It's time to just fully accept it and move on. You can't change your bone structure."

I grunted.

"Unfortunately."

Dominic was appalled. "You have an ass, a phat ass. I love it and so do the guys who check you out."

"No one checks me out."

Dominic snarled. "Trust me, they do. Why do you think I hate going into town with you? I have use bucket loads of self-control not to punch people."

I snorted. "And people say *I* have anger issues."

Dominic grinned. "I know I have a bad temper, but so do you. It's why we're a perfect match."

"A match made from Hell according to Branna."

"Like she can talk."

I chuckled and opened a bottle of Coke that Dominic handed to me. He had more chicken on his plate than I did because he could eat more, but I was curious as to why he was even eating this food in the first place.

"No celery sticks or steaks hidden in there?" I asked peering down into the picnic basket.

Dominic smirked. "Like I said, it's a one-time thing."

I sighed. "You will work all this off later, and I won't."

Dominic chewed on his lower lip before he released it and said, "You *could* work out with me, you know?"

I laughed but stopped when I saw Dominic's face.

"You can't be serious?"

Dominic gave me a stern look. "You have to look after your body, and I'm sorry to say it, but you're not fit, babe."

I frowned.

"I'm not calling you fat, before you go off at me. I'm just saying that it wouldn't hurt for you to be able to walk up stairs without losing your breath."

I was mortified because it was true.

I *was* very unfit.

I frowned. "You would ease me into it, right?"

Dominic's sudden smile warmed my heart—he was shocked that I was considering it.

"Of course I would, I'll do you up a beginner's exercise and diet program."

The word 'diet' disheartened me.

"I'm not eatin' rabbit food. You would be dead within a week after I turned into a monster and went on a rampage for real food."

Dominic burst out laughing. "You won't be eating rabbit food. You will eat the same food as me, just in smaller portions. You can still have small treats and even a cheat meal once a week."

Dominic got a cheat meal every week, and it was the Mega Meal Deal from Four Star Pizza. It was for a family of four, but he could finish it all by himself. We never had sex the night he had a cheat meal, but it seems to be worth it for him, even if he goes into a food coma after he eats it.

"Okay, fine. I'll do it... but not today. Monday."

Dominic nodded his head.

"Great, you could even try Pilates or something if you wanted."

On a diet?

"Are they allowed?"

Dominic furrowed his eyebrows. "It's an exercise, Bronagh. Pilates."

"*Pilates*? Oh, Jesus Christ, no. I thought you said *pie* and *lattes*."

Dominic looked at me like I grew an extra head, so I shrugged my shoulders and said, "I like food."

I smiled and then scooped up some beans onto three chips before I put them into my mouth to prove my point.

"You aren't going to use a fork... are you?"

I chewed and swallowed my food.

"To eat chips and chicken? Dude, no."

Dominic snarled, "Stop saying dude. I *don't* say dude!"

I swallowed my food and said, "Sorry, *bro*, it won't happen again."

"It's annoying that you can mimic my accent so perfectly now."

I snorted. "I listen to you yap on twenty-four-seven. Of course, I've picked it up."

Dominic mumbled something under his breath then proceeded to eat his food. I took a swig of my drink when I glanced to my left and smiled.

"Dominic," I whispered. "Look."

Dominic turned his head and followed my outstretched pointed finger to the lake that was twenty feet away from where we sat.

"That's a lot of ducklings."

I squealed a little. "They are so cute. I just want to squeeze them!"

Dominic's expression was unsure as he looked at me.

I cheerfully laughed. "I won't for real, don't worry."

I looked back to the mama duck and her babies as she waddled around and they followed her in a perfect line.

"Can you imagine if human kids followed their ma's around in a line like that?"

Dominic laughed. "It would be very amusing to see that."

I chuckled and continued to eat my food. After a few moments, I reached down into my bag and took out the book Dominic made me.

He chuckled. "You like it that much that you want to keep looking at it?"

I looked up and smiled. "I love it, you have no idea how much. I even love all the crude ones... But did you honestly have to say you love me because I give you head when I'm on my period?"

Dominic nodded his head. "Of course, you're so considerate during the week your period hits."

I burst out laughing.

He was such a weirdo.

"Well, I love it. It's the best present ever."

Dominic smirked. "You haven't received your third one yet."

Another present!

"Where is it?" I asked.

Dominic nodded to the bucket of chicken, so I leaned over and peered into the bucket. I felt my eyes widen when I saw a black rectangle box on the bottom of the bucket.

I felt my lower lip wobble then.

"You put my present under the chicken? You're so romantic."

Dominic laughed as I sniffled and reached into the bucket and lifted out my third birthday present.

"Thank you," I said to Dominic, who just nodded for me to open the box.

I took a breath then slowly lifted the lid of the box. I spotted the chain of a necklace first and I reached inside and lifted it out so I could see what the pendant was.

I stopped breathing when I caught a glimpse of the heart pendant. It wasn't just a normal flat heart shaped pendant—it had a hologram picture on the front and back.

"Me parents," I whispered as I slid my fingers over the holographic face of my beautiful mother then flipped it over to do the same to my father.

"I know how much you miss them and how much a part of your heart they are. I wanted something of them that you could carry around and keep close to your heart. Alannah helped me design it since she is great with designs and shit... Do you like it?"

Like didn't cover it.

"Words can't express—" I cut myself off as a sob escaped my throat.

"Baby, I didn't mean to make you cry so much on your birthday."

"Stop givin' me priceless presents that I adore, then!" I snapped through my tears and crawled over to him.

Dominic only smiled at me and opened his arms. I wrapped my arms around his neck and my legs around his hips as I sat on him.

"You're the best thing that has ever happened to me. I'm so glad you sat on me chair in school."

Dominic vibrated with laughter as he squeezed me tight.

"Me too, pretty girl, me too."

I leaned back and handed my chain to him. He smiled and lifted the chain over my head and fixed the heart on my chest.

"You look like your dad, you know? I went through loads of pictures to find clear ones that could be made visible on your pendant, and I was a little shocked at how much you resemble him. You have his eyes, nose, and ears, but your mom's smile. They would be so proud of you."

Oh, fuck him anyway.

I started sobbing again so Dominic silently hugged me and rocked me from side to side.

"I'm happy that I didn't wear any makeup today."

"Me, too. My shirt would look like a colouring book if you had."

I giggled and continued to hug him tightly. I released him then and moved back over to my side of the blanket. We finished our food, and to be honest, it made me a little tired. I opened my mouth and yawned, but before I could fully enjoy it, Dominic stuck his fingers in my mouth and said, "Yawn rape."

Oh, for fuck's sake.

"Will you *stop* doin' that?"

"No."

"But it drives me mad!"

"I know."

"So, stop it!"

"No."

Gah!

I screeched in frustration like a child and flopped onto my back and laid still.

I heard Dominic sigh. "Bronagh, grow up. You're twenty-one, act like it."

I chewed my inner cheeks and stayed put. I heard Dominic as he packed everything up, but I wouldn't look up to see. His face appeared over mine after a few minutes, and the bastard, as usual, was smiling.

"Come on, child. We have one more thing to do before we go home."

I wanted to lie down and not move for at least half an hour.

"What's in it for me?" I mumbled.

"Your fourth present."

Oh... well played, Mr. Slater, well played.

"Okay fine, help me up. But I'm not talkin' to you because you stuck your fingers in me mouth. That shite is just fuckin' nasty."

Dominic laughed and helped me to my feet. He pulled out his phone then and unexpectedly kissed me and took a picture of it. I laughed, and he snapped that picture, too.

"Okay, pull a stupid face."

I went cross-eyed and stuck my tongue out while Dominic pulled a silly face, too.

"Why all the pictures?"

Dominic grinned. "You'll see.... now are you ready for your fourth present?"

I smirked. "Born ready."

Chapter Five

"Bowlin'? You're takin' me *bowlin'* for a birthday present... Thank you, but really?"

Dominic grinned. "Bowling itself isn't the present. You get your present at the end of the game."

He sat down at the control panel of our bowling lane and typed in our names. He typed in Nico as player one and Phat Ass as player two.

"No!" I snapped, but before I could change it, the fucker hit the enter button and started the game. "You're evil."

Dominic grinned and stood up; he rolled his head on his shoulders and his neck cracked. I instantly put my hands to my ears and sang so I wouldn't hear the cracking sound. I jumped when Dominic smacked my arse as he passed by me to select a bowling ball.

He stared down at a range of different coloured balls, and after a minute of thought, he settled on the red one. I wasn't surprised because red was his favourite colour.

"You aren't allowed to let me win—this is a serious game."

Dominic looked to me and winked. "You're going down, baby."

"Down on you? I hope so."

Dominic's heated gaze bored into mine, and it made me grin.

I waved him on. "Go on, show me what you can do."

Dominic turned his back to me as he stepped towards our lane. With his bowling ball in hand, he swung his arm back then forward and released the ball. I sat up in my seat and watched as the ball zoomed down the lane at lightning speed and smacked the pins bang on in the middle. The force of the hit caused all of the pins to be knocked down.

"STRIKE!" the machine roared.

"Goddammit," I muttered and stood up to take my turn.

Dominic walked by me looking smug as fuck.

Bastard.

I walked over to the bowling balls and selected a purple one, and I had to hold it with both hands because it was a little heavy.

"You can do this," I said to myself as I stepped forward to our lane.

I glanced to my right just as a little kid three lanes away rolled his ball down the lane and knocked all his pins down.

Every. Single. Pin.

He couldn't have been older than nine, ten at the most.

If he can do this, so can I.

I nodded my head and swung my arm backwards, but I screeched when the ball flew out of my hand. I quickly turned and scrambled after it.

"It's okay, it's okay. Nothin' was broken. I have it under control. Nothin' to see here folks," I called out to the staff members who stared at me and shook their heads.

I looked at Dominic, who took up two seats because he fell to his side from laughing so hard.

"Shut the fuck up. You're makin' a scene."

"The scene," Dominic laughed, "was made when you decided to throw a bowling ball in the air."

I huffed.

"It slipped out of me hand... and nothin' was broken so give it a rest."

He continued to laugh. "I wish I'd recorded that."

Fucking fuckface.

I angrily turned and stepped up to our lane. I gripped the ball tighter this time and swung my arm back then forward to release it down my lane but the same thing happened, it went up into the fucking air then landed back down on the ground with a terrifying thud.

"Oh, please, *stop*. I can't breathe!"

I'll cut that hyena's breathing off for good if he keeps laughing at me.

I jumped backwards from the ball that had just crashed onto the floor, then in annoyance I put my foot behind the ball and pushed as hard as I could. It worked, the ball went gliding down the lane and I jumped up and down with excitement.

It crashed into the pins and knocked a few of them down.

I turned and punched the air.

"Yes."

Dominic shook his head at me. "That's cheating."

Oh, Mr. Proper.

"Whatever, how many did I knock down?"

"Six pins."

I did a little hip thrust dance. "Yeah, boy."

Dominic shook his head at me as he stood up.

"Let me show you how it's done."

I rolled my eyes. "You're pickin' things I've never done before for these birthday dates. The only one I've been good at so far is eatin' chicken at our picnic."

Dominic tilted his head at me. "You've never gone bowling before?"

I deadpanned. "Did you not see my first two attempts at tryin' to roll the ball down the lane?"

"Yeah, but I thought that was just because you sucked."

Oh.

"Thanks very bloody much!"

Dominic held up his hands. "Just telling you the truth."

I narrowed my eyes and said, "Game on, fuckface."

I turned and walked to the control panel for our game and watched the screen.

Dominic raised his eyebrows at me, then turned, got his red ball from the ball machine and walked to our lane. He rolled it down the lane and got another strike.

Fuck.

He walked back and sat next to me, a grin tugging at his lips.

I grunted as I stood up. "Don't smile just yet."

He turned his head from me as I rolled my neck on my shoulders and shook out my hands. I was going to roll a ball down that fucking lane, even if it killed me.

"Okay," I breathed.

I got my purple ball from the ball machine and walked up to the line that separated me from the lane.

"Be with one with the ball," I said.

Dominic cracked up behind me. "You okay there, Yoda?"

I was going to harm him badly if he didn't close his mouth.

"I'm concentratin'!"

"Sorry."

He wasn't sorry.

I shook off Dominic and focused.

You can do this.

I went old school and spread my legs, bent down and rolled the ball from between my legs down the lane. It didn't have much power behind it, but it was rolling down the lane instead of possibly flying at a person's face. To me that was a success.

"To the right," I mumbled and motioned the ball to go to the right with my hands.

"That's it, use the air to push the ball in the right direction."

I gave Dominic the finger.

"Yes!" I jumped when the ball knocked into the pins.

I quickly walked back to Dominic.

"How many was that?" I asked.

"Two pins."

Two.

Fucking two?

"That's bollocks."

Maybe I should just kick all the balls down the lane. I knocked a lot of pins down the first time I did that.

I sighed and looked at Dominic. The level of smugness on that lad's face was unreal. He thought he was so bloody cool beating a girl at a game.

"Pussy," I mumbled.

"What was that?" Dominic asked.

"I called you a pussy. A p-u-s-s-y. Pussy."

Dominic's jaw dropped. "How am I a pussy?"

I shrugged. "Your smugness is annoyin' me. You think you're all that and packet of Tayto crisps 'cause you're winnin' at bowlin'. Let's go home and play chess. I'd fuckin' *destroy* you at chess."

Dominic pretended to be scared. "Not chess, *anything* but chess."

"You know what? I'm not dealin' with your sarcastic self today —it's my birthday, bitch. I'm twenty-one. It's *my* day, not yours, so screw you."

I would have loved if my hair were down so I could flip it, it was a perfect fuck you hair-flip moment.

"Ohhh, this really is an 'it's my birthday and I'll cry if I want to' type of day you're havin'. I'll take you in a mood with me over cryin', though."

I reached forward and shoved Dominic in the chest.

"I can't help it if I'm soft hearted and cry easily, okay? If I were hard-hearted, I would have never dated your stupid Yank arse."

Dominic smirked. "You aren't insulting me."

Dammit.

"I'm never comin' here with you again. I hope you know that."

Dominic shrugged. "I won't be bringin' you back here again. You suck even worse than Branna does, and she is a complete girl when it comes to sports."

Okay, that does it. I wasn't talking to him!

I gave him the finger then sat down and folded my arms across my chest. Dominic snorted as he went and bowled another bloody strike. This continued for the rest of the stupid game. Dominic got a strike, spare, or knocked a lot of the pins down. I, on the other hand, knocked down three or four pins during each turn. Five, if I was lucky.

Dominic was right.

I sucked.

I wasn't admitting that out loud to the bastard, though.

"Grumpy gills, it's your final turn."

I grumbled as I stood up. "Your score is one hundred and three, mine is twenty-three... I think we both know you've won."

Dominic smirked. "Just go bowl your final turn."

I did, but I did it with an attitude.

I was about to throw my ball when a woman my age appeared next to me. She was a little taller than me with white-blond, hip length hair and big blue eyes.

She was very pretty.

"Hey, I'm Jo."

I smiled. "Bronagh."

"I hope you don't mind me sayin', but you're doin' that all wrong. I couldn't help but notice your form, and since your brother won't help you, I will."

My brother.

She thinks Dominic is my brother?

I mentally rolled my eyes because this happened so bloody often to me.

I got it, okay! Dominic was incredibly hot, and I was the homely girlfriend who fit better as his sibling rather than his partner.

Whatever.

I decided to humour the girl because I needed all the help I could get. I looked over my shoulder to Dominic and smiled.

"Jo here is goin' to help me with me form because you, dear *brother*, won't."

I could see the amusement on Dominic's face as he waved me on.

I turned back to Jo and said, "Teach me, oh wise one."

Jo smiled and moved behind me; she reached forward and touched my hand then placed her left hand on my hip to steady me or something.

"Okay, keep your body straight, draw your arm back and swing, but no so hard that you knock yourself off balance. I've watched you, and you move your whole body forward when you throw the ball. Only move your throwing arm, keep the rest of your body straight."

Oh.

That explains why I messed up so bad on my first two attempts at throwing the ball.

"Okay, so pull back... swing forward... and release."

I did as Jo said, and I felt as though the entire bowling alley was watching the ball zoom down the lane.

I jumped up and down when the machine voice shouted, "STRIKE!"

I got a strike.

I fucking got one.

"Yes!" I screamed and instantly turned and hugged Jo, who hugged me back and jumped up and down with me.

I pulled back to thank her and the weirdest thing happened.

She kissed me.

She. Kissed. Me.

"You're welcome, enjoy the rest of your game." Jo beamed then turned and walked off like she didn't just kiss me on the mouth.

I blinked a couple of times then turned back to Dominic with my mouth open and found him laughing his head off with his phone pointed in my direction.

Is that motherfucker recording me?

"Delete it!" I growled and wiped my mouth.

Dominic quickly tapped on the screen of his phone then jumped up. "Too late. My brothers, your sister, and Alannah have now seen you get hit on and kissed by a girl."

I was red with embarrassment.

"You bastard, why would you do that?"

"Because that was the funniest shit I've ever seen in my entire life. That girl looked at your ass more than she did your face. She was literally eye fucking it."

Will the mortification ever stop?

"I'm leavin'!"

Dominic jumped up and put his arms around my body as he stopped me from walking away.

"The game isn't over yet."

Really?

"I've played enough bowlin' to last me a lifetime."

"What about your present, though?"

Oh, that bastard.

"I've done what you asked—I played the game... now where is it?"

Dominic chuckled. "Um... it's down the end of our lane."

Come again?

"Excuse me?"

"I made you work for your other presents, what's different about this one?"

I groaned in annoyance.

"What happened to just handin' someone a present and sayin' here you go, happy birthday?"

"That's boring."

I rolled my eyes. "That's one thing you aren't. This day has exhausted me, and it's only after five. What *you* think is excitin' is not *my* idea of excitin'."

Dominic sighed. "Just go get your present, I promise this one will be the most exciting part of your day."

Oh?

"I've to walk down the lane? Will I not get in trouble?"

Dominic laughed. "No, who will say something to you?"

"Uh, the staff."

"Ryder came and put the present down at the end of our lane. He told them what was going on."

I swallowed. "And they just agreed?"

Dominic shrugged. "Would you disagree with Ryder?"

"I disagree with 'em all the time."

"Bad example, you don't fear me and my brothers, but most people do. The staff won't say anything and if they do, I'll have a word with them."

Oh, scary man.

"Fine, let me go so I can get this done."

Dominic released me, smacked my arse, and sent me on my way.

I walked to the lane and stepped onto the walking strip that the staff must use so they don't fall. I walked all the way down to where the pins were lined up and hunkered down.

"Where the fuck is me present?" I mumbled.

I bent all the way down until I was lying on my stomach and looking under the pin machine. I saw a blue and silver rope with a collar at the end of it.

A lead?

I reached for it, but my arms were too short to grab it. I carefully moved onto the slippery lane and moved closer to the pins. I reached to the side and grabbed the lead with my hand then I got to my feet.

I examined the lead with confused eyes. I looked at the collar then at the blank tag that was shaped like a doggie bone.

A dog?

"Why would he buy me a lead if we don't have a—Omigod!"

I turned to Dominic.

"You got me a dog?" I screamed.

He was standing on the end of the lane and recording me again on his phone.

"I got you a dog."

Oh, my God!

I screamed in delight then jumped up and down but jumping up and down on a bowling alley lane was *not* a smart move.

Seriously, don't ever do it.

I slipped and fell back on my arse, crashing into the pins and knocking them all down. I groaned and rolled out of the way just as the pin machine came down to scoop the pins away.

"That hurt," I groaned and crawled out to the path I used to walk down the lane.

I stood up, put my hand on my arse, and began walking back towards Dominic. I looked up and glared at him. He was on his knees recording me, but he was laughing.

"That wasn't funny."

I noticed Dominic was crying when I reached him.

Crying with laughter.

"That was hilarious."

Bastard.

"I think I broke me arse."

Dominic stood up and gave me a tight hug. "There is never a dull moment with you, pretty girl."

I grunted. "So happy to amuse you."

Dominic pulled back and snorted. "You got a strike when you knocked all the pins down with your ass."

Typical, fucking typical.

"It was worth it. You got me a dog!"

Dominic gave my head a kiss. "I got you a dog."

"Where?"

He grinned. "At home."

"What are we still here for then? Let's go!"

Chapter Six

"**B**ranna?" I screamed when I opened the door to my house.
"Don't shout, you will scare him."
Him.

"Branna?" I whispered as I rid myself of my cardigan and dolly shoes.

I checked the sitting room first, but it was empty. Next up was the kitchen, but it was empty, too.

"Hey, birthday girl, do I get a kiss from you like that chick at the bowling alley did?"

Ryder, Kane, *and* Alec were in the kitchen, but no puppy and my puppy was all I wanted to see.

I ignored Alec's nasty self.

"Branna?" I called out.

"She's out in the backyard—"

"Branna!" I squealed as I ran to the back door and looked through the glass.

I spotted Branna sitting on the ground while a chubby little Siberian Husky sat next to her.

Dominic got me a Siberian Husky.

I screamed *and* jumped up and down.

"Oh, my God!" I cried.

I pulled the sliding door open just as Dominic said, "She hasn't stopped crying all day."

I was so happy with every present he got me, how could I *not* cry?

"There's Mama," Branna beamed up at me.

I slowly walked over before I sunk to my knees and then lay down on my belly and rested my head on my hands.

"Hello," I whispered to the puppy as he waddled over to my face.

I laughed when he licked my nose.

"He loves you already," I heard Dominic say from behind me.

"I love him already, too," I sniffled.

I sat up then and lifted him into my arms, holding him to my chest.

"What do you want to call him?" Dominic asked.

I lifted the puppy up and looked into his bright blue, gorgeous eyes.

"How about... Tyson?"

I heard murmurs of approval then Dominic said, "I like Tyson."

Tyson.

"Your name is Tyson."

I kissed Tyson's head and then put him on the ground. I used my arms to wipe my tears from my face then crawled over to Branna and lifted up my necklace.

"Look."

Branna took my pendant in her hand. She looked at both sides of the heart and then burst into tears. I instantly started crying right along with her, and it caused a round of mumbling from behind us.

"I'm getting bee some water," Kane's voice murmured. "If she has been crying like this all day the girl must be getting dehydrated."

He was so thoughtful!

I calmed myself down and hugged my sister tightly.

"He made me a cool book, too," I whispered. "I'll show you it later, though."

Branna smiled, wiped her eyes, then nodded her head.

I looked back down at Tyson when he decided to gnaw on the end of my dress. I smiled and tugged my dress from him. I lightly tapped his nose and firmly said, "No."

I was going to nip any chewing and eating of clothes directly in the bud, immediately. I stood up then bent down and picked Tyson up into my arms.

"I love him so much!" I turned to Dominic, Ryder, and Alec as I held Tyson out for them to see. "Just look at him. Isn't he gorgeous?"

"Beautiful."

"Fabulous."

"Stunning."

I glared at the three of them. Sarcasm radiated off them in waves.

I looked at Tyson. "They are mutts, so don't mind them, baby."

"*Mutts*?"

I smirked. "Mutts."

Alec glared at me. "I'm offended."

"Good."

I looked away and smiled.

"Dinner will be done soon. I've had it on the past hour."

I looked to Branna. "Me and Dominic already had food... but I could eat."

I looked to Dominic who was staring at me.

Diet and exercise starts Monday, not today!

I rolled my eyes. "Me arse can't get any bigger. Give me a break."

Alec tilted to the side and looked down to my behind. "So squat more and it will."

I laughed. "I'm not *tryin'* to make it bigger. It's big enough as it is."

"The bigger, the better I say," Dominic said.

Alec shrugged his shoulders. "I appreciate a nice ass as much as you do, bro, but I'm more of a leg man."

I laughed. "Yeah, because that's the first part of a male underwear model you look at... their legs."

Ryder walked into the house laughing and Dominic quickly followed not wanting to listen or take part in the conversation anymore.

"Okay, when it comes to *women,* I'm a leg man, but for men, I'm a straight-up cock lover."

I bent over because I was laughing so hard.

"You're so disgustin' that it's funny!"

Alec grinned.

I continued to laugh as we walked back into my house. I held Tyson tight to my chest and looked at Dominic.

"You're gonna have to build him two houses."

Dominic frowned. "Why two?"

"So, he can have his own house out in our back and one out your brother's back. Duh."

"Fine, I'll get on that soon."

"Tomorrow."

Dominic rolled his eyes. "Fine, tomorrow."

I smiled in victory and snuggled Tyson. "You're gonna be so spoiled."

Ryder laughed and said to Dominic, "You know you've just knocked yourself down to number two on her list of priorities, right?"

"What are you talking about?"

"Bronagh will put Tyson's needs before yours from now on."

"That's not true."

It is so true.

"Babe, that's not true... right?"

I shrugged. "He is a puppy and he needs me—he needs *us*—to help him until he gets bigger. He comes first since he is dependent on us."

Dominic was horrified. "What have I done?"

"You have limited the amount of pus-say you're going to get on a weekly basis, *that* is what you have done."

Dominic growled, "I get some every day, sometimes *more* than once. That won't change."

Kane smirked at his brother. "If you're trying to get some and Tyson cries at night, bumble bee will be out of your bed so fast your head will spin... and not in a good way."

I snickered.

"We really should have called him cock blocker," Alec murmured, making Branna and me burst out laughing.

"Everyone, sit down at the table," Branna chuckled. "Dinner is done."

I put a now sleeping Tyson down onto a brand new doggie bed. He was so tiny on the big bed. I found a new teddy that was bought for him and put it in next to him, as well. My heart exploded when Tyson yawned and put his paw on the teddy and snuggled it to his body.

"Oh, my God!" I whispered and jumped up and down on the spot. "I love him so much."

Arms came around me from behind.

"More than me?"

Right now, that was questionable.

I turned to Dominic and smiled as I leaned in and whispered, "When we're alone, you can have me arse."

Dominic's hold tightened almost painfully around me.

"Lovebirds, food time."

Dominic growled as I pulled away and led him to the kitchen table with a big grin on my face.

"The only thing I want to eat is you," Dominic growled as we sat down.

I gasped. "Not now!"

Alec looked at Dominic with a horrified expression. "Don't talk like that about her… I get a strong urge to punch you when you do."

I grinned.

Alec and the other brothers had developed a big brother bond with me, and it usually meant hell for Dominic.

"Leave me be," Dominic snarled.

Alec narrowed his eyes. "Imagine me doing a naked dance as I swing my cock around like a helicopter."

I burst into laughter.

Dominic heaved. "What the fuck, bro?"

Alec smiled and looked to me. "You can eat your food in peace, he won't get a hard on for a few more hours until that image leaves his mind."

"Correct me if I'm wrong, but didn't you say you would wash the delph after the match was over, Dominic?"

Dominic looked at me when I spoke, and so did his brothers.

"Don't correct her, you won't wake up tomorrow morning if you do," Kane murmured to Dominic then took a swig from his bottle of Bulmers.

Dominic glanced at his brother then looked back to me with a smirk on his face. "Damn, pretty girl, you're looking mighty fine in that apron."

I looked down at Branna's Minnie Mouse apron then back up at Dominic with a scowl on my face.

"That was a pathetic attempt to distract me."

Kane snorted. "She knows you like the back of her hand. You're going to have to come up with some new material."

Dominic ignored Kane and kept his eyes on me. "The game just ended. I'll wash the *dishes* later."

I rolled my eyes.

He hated when I said delph instead of dishes.

I raised my eyebrows. "Oh, you'll get to it later, will you?"

Alec leaned into Dominic. "It's a trap. Don't answer her, just smile."

Dominic's face lit up with a charming smile that would cause both men and women to stop and stare. I would have been caught up in staring at his dimples if I hadn't heard what Alec had just said.

I wasn't backing down on this—I was no one's maid!

"Branna cooked the dinner for you all, and I then cleared everythin' away afterwards. You lost the coin toss, Dominic, so come help us."

He remained quiet.

"Dominic," I said my tone firm.

His smile never faltered. "Yes?"

I folded my arms across my chest. "It's later, get up and go wash the *delph*."

Dominic dropped his smile and glanced at his brothers who were each hiding a smile behind their bottles of beer. "If I get up and do what you're asking me to, my brothers will think I'm a bitch."

I shrugged. "And if you don't get up and do as you're *told*, you will fully understand the term blue balls because you won't get any for a month."

"Being called a bitch it is, then," Dominic chirped then stood up and headed in my direction. He winked at me as he passed me then went down the hall and into the kitchen.

"What have you done to our brother?" Ryder asked me with a big smile on his face.

I shrugged. "I have him in trainin'."

"Training? What is he training for?" Alec asked.

I smirked as I looked at Ryder, Alec, then Kane.

"Marriage."

Each of them shuddered then laughed like what I said was hilarious.

It made me smile. They could laugh all the wanted, marriage was in the cards for all of them. Every girlfriend they had ever had and will ever have was training them... they just didn't know it.

Chapter Seven

"Dominic."

"What?"

I grinned as I tightened the silk robe around my body. "Come here," I called.

I could hear him sigh. "I'm watching a movie with Tyson."

Oh God, it begins.

"I have a surprise for *you*."

Boy, do I have a surprise.

I glanced at my wall and gazed at the new canvas on it. Dominic brought it into our room a little while ago and said it was just made before he collected my fifth present. I had no idea what he was talkin' about until I removed the cover and saw every picture Dominic took of us throughout the day, he said he forwarded each picture he took of us to a friend so they could create the canvas. I, of course, cried when I saw it, but now it just makes me smile.

I grinned when I heard footsteps coming up the stairs then down the hallway until they halted outside our bedroom doorway.

"A surprise for me? But it's *your* birthday."

I grinned. "True, but you gave me so much today, and I wanted to give you somethin' back."

Dominic glanced around the room and stepped inside.

"What is it?"

I smiled and undid the knot on my robe and let the material fall away from my body.

"Jesus fucking Christ."

I smirked as I slowly walked towards Dominic, who was frozen as he watched me.

"You like?" I asked, turning around.

The hiss that came from his mouth when his eyes landed on my arse sent a thrill throughout my body.

"Baby," he breathed. "Where did you get that?"

He was referring to the lingerie I was wearing.

"Branna got it for me birthday. I figured I would put it to good use."

The lingerie was made up of a black camisole top that connected to the suspenders on the high thigh stockings I was also wearing. Everything matched, even the black booty shorts. Everything except the bright red heels I was wearing... I had to add Dominic's favourite colour somewhere.

"The colour of the lingerie against your pale skin is just.... perfection," he whispered.

I lowered my head and smiled.

He took a step forward and then gripped the hem of his t-shirt and pulled it from his body revealing his sculpted chest and stomach.

Christ.

I swallowed and playfully took a step back.

Dominic smirked. "What? You're going to make me work for it?"

I raised an eyebrow. "You've made me work all day... this is only fair."

I backed up all the way to the bed when Dominic pulled down his tracksuit bottoms leaving him in just his boxers.

His *very tented* boxers.

Dominic licked his lips. "You have no idea what you do to me, Bronagh."

I looked to his boxers and murmured, "I have an idea."

I flicked my eyes up and my mouth watered. His V line and abs were drool worthy.

"I can't believe all that is mine." I swallowed as I stared at Dominic's body.

I watched in a trance as Dominic's body came closer to mine. When he was close enough to do so, he put his arms around me and slid them down to my behind.

"And I can't believe all *this* is mine."

I hissed as he squeezed my behind.

"Easy, tiger, it's tender from when I fell today."

Dominic kissed my shoulder and pushed his hands up under my camisole and flattened his palms against my skin.

"You're so soft," he murmured.

I closed my eyes as he turned his head and placed his mouth on my neck. He found my sweet spot straight away and sucked. I giggled because it tickled and gave me goosebumps.

"You never last more than a few seconds before you laugh when I kiss your neck."

I pulled back and shrugged. "It's ticklish."

Dominic tried to place his mouth back on my sweet spot, but I burst into a fit of giggles and fell back onto the bed in an effort to get away from his mouth. Dominic followed me down onto the bed and hovered over me.

"You're on top this time, I'm not missing a single inch of you in that outfit. I'm lying back and enjoying the hell out of this ride."

I laughed as Dominic got up then jumped onto the bed and lay down flat. He rid himself of his underwear and gripped his cock in his hand and stroked.

"Stand at the end of the bed and crawl to me, baby."

I stood up and moved to the end of the bed. I kept eye contact with him as I put my hands on the end of the bed followed by my knees.

"Slower," Dominic whispered.

He continued to stroke himself as he watched me.

It was hot.

I slowly put one limb in front of the next as I crawled up the bed. I paused for a moment then reached up and removed the spider grip from my hair allowing it to fall down in waves.

"Fuck," Dominic hissed.

I placed my hands on his thighs and lowered my head to his groin. I nudged his hand away from his cock with my head and licked it from the base to tip.

"Mine," I purred.

Dominic bucked a little up into my face at my declaration.

"Put me in your mouth... That's it. Yesss."

I pulled my hair to one side as I worked my mouth on Dominic's cock. I took hold of his length and stroked it in time with my mouth.

"Fuck, Bronagh!"

I hummed around Dominic, and he growled in response.

"Ride me, baby. I won't last long tonight."

I smiled and released Dominic with a pop. I crawled up his body then sat down and slowly ground my pussy against his length.

"Fuck! How can I feel—Are they *crotchless*?"

I smirked and nodded my head.

"Christ, put me inside you. I *really* won't last long tonight, you look so fucking hot."

I smiled as I reached down and guided Dominic into my body.

"Daddy's home," he growled as I sunk down and took his entire length.

I placed my hands on Dominic's chest and pushed myself up then sunk back down.

Yes.

I tilted my head back and groaned.

Dominic reached up and palmed my breasts through my camisole before he moved his hands down to my hips so he could hold on as he pumped up into me.

"You are so fucking sexy," he growled and moved his thumb around to the front of my body.

He found my clit and rubbed.

Oh, God.

"Come on, baby," Dominic urged.

I picked up my pace as I sunk down on his length and he trusted upwards into my body.

"Yes!" I cried out.

I continued to bounce on Dominic until his fingers on my clit caused my lower half to twitch. Dominic sat up, put his arms around me then rolled me under him. He continued to pound in and out of me while I moved my fingers to my clit and finished the job he started.

"Quick, Bronagh!" Dominic shouted.

I rubbed my clit as fast as I could and pulses erupted throughout my body causing my back to arch and my eyes to roll back.

I heard Dominic's loud groan, but I didn't react to him or open my eyes for a minute or two after the pulses stopped.

Dominic rolled off me and onto his side.

"You turn me out every single time."

I didn't know what that meant, but it sounded good so I was pleased.

"Was that me sixth present?" I asked Dominic.

"Yeah... you're welcome."

I laughed and turned on my side, hugging him.

"Today has been me best birthday ever. Thank you."

"You're welcome, my love."

I smiled, closed my eyes, and in seconds, I was out.

"Damien? Hi!"

I heard the smile in Damien's voice. "Hey bee, happy birthday!"

I beamed and adjusted my phone on my ear. "Thank you! How are you? I miss you!"

"I miss you, too, and I'm fine, doing good."

I frowned. "Come home, then."

Damien sighed. "Bronagh."

"I know, I know... you need to 'find yourself'. What does that even mean anyway?"

Damien laughed. "It means that I can't go somewhere where I'll mess up people I care about while I fix my head."

But it's been almost three years.

"Are you close to fixin' yourself?"

Damien mumbled, "I'm getting there."

That is better than nothing.

"How are my stupid brothers?"

I grinned. "Have you not called them today?"

"I have, but I want to hear the crap they have been getting up to from you."

I laughed. "Same old, same old. Ryder and Branna are in love, Alec is a slut and loves himself, Kane is still going on about buyin' the community centre and me and Dominic are... me and Dominic."

Damien laughed. "It's good to know that some things will never change."

Ain't that the truth.

"How's Alannah?"

I smiled. "She's good. She is in her final year in college doin' graphic design, as you know. You should see the things she does. She has her own website now, and she designs loads of things like book covers, websites, banners, logos. Any graphic you can think of she can do and all her designs are original. She is wicked good at drawin' them out and then usin' all her gadgets to scan them onto a computer. She is makin' a livin' with it, too. She is happy."

"Good," Damien said. "I'm happy for her, she deserves it."

I smiled. "She asks about you, too, you know."

"She does?" Damien asked then cleared his voice. "I mean, she does? That's nice."

I laughed. "Cut the act with me. I know you both still have the hots for each other."

"The 'hots' was never the problem with us, it was me."

I frowned. "Dame, you made a mistake. Stop beatin' yourself —"

"I've got to go, Bronagh. My break is over."

I frowned.

He was a night guard in a business firm building.

"Okay, I'll talk to you soon. Stay safe. I love you."

"Love you, too, bee. Bye, baby."

I frowned and lay back on my bed.

Dominic entered the room a few minutes later and asked what was wrong.

"I was on the phone with Damien. I miss him."

Dominic looked down. "Me, too."

I knew he missed him.

Dominic and Damien were twins, and up until Damien left, the pair was inseparable.

"He'll be home soon."

"When is soon?" I asked.

Dominic shrugged. "Eventually,"

Great.

I sighed but stopped and looked at Dominic. "Why are you all dressed up?"

Dominic grinned. "We're all going out for your birthday drinks."

"Who is goin'?"

"My brothers, Branna, Aideen, and I think her friend, Keela."

I frowned. "Not Alannah or Gavin?"

Dominic shook his head. "Gavin is working, and yes, I called him, and Alannah has… girl pains. I don't know much else because I hung up on her."

I laughed. "Does talkin' about cramps make you uncomfortable?"

"Yes," Dominic instantly replied.

I laughed and stood up. "I don't know what to wear."

Dominic looked at me and swallowed. "Leave the lingerie on, put any dress on over it, but don't take it off."

I felt my pulse spike. "Okay."

Dominic grinned. "Hurry up, everyone is coming here then we're taking a cab."

"Where are we goin'?"

"You'll see."

Chapter Eight

Playhouse nightclub.
That was where we ended up going for my birthday celebration.

I've been to Playhouse a few times. It was a good club, just not a normal club. It was a legal version of Darkness. There were brawls and all sorts of fights held in Playhouse for money prizes, and it was completely legit.

People loved it.

I didn't mind it because Dominic rarely partook in the fights. When people knew he was fighting, the only people who would fight him were those who were drunk and brave or lads who had never heard of him before.

What I did mind were the girl fights.

Yeah, *female* fights.

I was not sexist in any way. I strongly believed women could do whatever a man could. But there was something very off-putting about watching two girls kick the shite out of each other up on the platform for a money prize—but hey, to each their own.

"What is the event tonight?" I leaned over and asked Dominic as we sat down around a large table.

Dominic shrugged his shoulders.

I eyed him. "Are you fightin'?"

He chuckled. "No, it's your birthday. I'm spendin' my time with you, not up on the platform."

Good, that was good.

I smiled and looked at Branna as she walked back from the bar with drinks. She handed me a cocktail.

"It's a Blowjob," she shouted.

All the males at the table suddenly paid attention to Branna and she laughed.

"Bronagh's *drink* is a called Blowjob."

Everyone laughed.

Dominic leaned into me as I took a sip of my drink and said, "You swallow that Blowjob like a good girl."

I almost choked.

I coughed and rubbed my chest while Dominic waggled his eyebrows at me.

He was such a man.

I looked at Branna, who was dancing in her seat since Ryder was talking to his friends. I smiled and stood up and reached for her hand.

"Dance?"

She didn't reply, she just jumped up and grabbed my hand then pulled me to the dance floor.

We jumped around like fools to "Gangnam Style" and almost broke our necks when we tripped over our heels, but instead of sitting down, we laughed and continued to dance around.

I jumped in shock when I felt hands on my hips. I looked over my shoulder and shook my head at the lad who was trying to dance on me.

"I have a boyfriend, sorry."

The lad smiled. "No worries."

He continued to dance and pulled my behind into his groin. I pushed away from him and turned around.

"I don't want to dance with you."

The lad shook his head. "Prick tease."

Wait, what?

I am dancing to "Gangnam Style," how is that being a prick tease?

I glared at the lad then grabbed Branna's hand and made a move to walk by him, but he smiled and moved in front of me.

"Move, please," Branna said, her tone firm.

The lad only smirked.

She glared at the lad then looked at me. "I'll be right back."

The lad let her by and focused back on me. I was shoved into him when people dancing behind me knocked me forward. The lad who was being a nuisance put his arms around me.

"Let go!" I snapped.

He laughed.

"Me sister is gone to get me fella and he will hurt you, so just let me go!"

He moved a hand down to my arse and squeezed.

"It's real," he murmured in my ear.

Of course, it is fucking real... did it look fake or something?

I shoved and tried to hit the lad, but he grabbed my hand and leaned his head down to mine. This fool actually tried to kiss me.

I pulled my head back as far as I could then without warning I fell back and landed on the ground with a thud.

Oh, God.

Pain.

"Bronagh!" I heard Branna's voice over the music.

I felt her hands on me as she pulled me up to my feet. I steadied myself and leaned forward to try and ease some of the pain in my arse.

I fell exactly on the same spot I had hurt in the bowlin' alley earlier.

There was going to be one hell of a bruise on that spot.

"Fuck," I grunted.

"Are you okay?" Branna asked.

I nodded my head and looked past Branna when I saw an arm rise up in the air then swing down. I lowered my gaze and widened my eyes.

"Kane, stop!"

I expected to see Dominic kicking the lad's arse, but it was Kane, and my God, he had the fella bloodied up good.

Dominic and Ryder suddenly appeared behind Kane, and they each grabbed hold of him and pulled him off the lad who was writhing around on the floor in pain.

I grimaced when I seen his bloody face.

I was pretty sure Kane broke his nose.

Dominic got in Kane's face and shouted at him. Kane shouted back and pointed to the lad and then to me.

Dominic looked at me then to the lad on the ground.

I flinched when Dominic kicked the lad in the stomach then got down to eye level and shouted something into his face.

He got up just as the club's bouncers showed up.

He walked up to them and leaned in close so they could hear him over the music. He pointed to the lad on the floor then pointed to me. The bouncers nodded their heads then moved to the lad on the floor, picked him up, and carried him off somewhere.

I instantly moved towards Dominic when he held his hand out to me. Branna walked ahead of me with Ryder and Kane while I hung back with Dominic.

"Are you okay?"

I shrugged.

"He hurt you?"

I shook my head.

"Then what?"

I sighed. "He squeezed me arse and seemed surprised that it was real."

Dominic looked at me with raised eyebrows. "You aren't upset that a stranger practically molested you. You're upset that said stranger thought your ass was fake?"

Damn.

"I've been with you so long that serious things are startin' to take a backseat to stupid problems."

Dominic shook his head. "You're crazy."

I smiled as we got back to our table then I leaned over and hugged Kane and said thank you.

"You okay?" he asked.

I nodded my head. "Me arse broke me fall."

Kane chortled.

I took a drink from Dominic's outstretched hand and began sipping on it. We all chatted for a few minutes until a loud female from our left got Branna's attention.

"Aideen!" she screeched.

I turned my head and watched as Aideen Collins walked towards us in a tight fitting blue dress that her tits almost fell out of.

She owned a serious set of boobs.

"Who the fuck is *that*?" Kane asked and stared at Aideen with his mouth agape.

I smiled at his facial expression. "Aideen Collins... Gavin's older sister."

"*That* is Gavin's older sister? Fuck me, she is hot."

I rolled my eyes at his wording, but I had to agree with him. Aideen *was* stunning. She was old friends with Branna and was Irish to the core. She was common as hell, a true Dub—but the girl wasn't pale, she was lightly tanned. Like her brother, Gavin, whenever the sun came out, she naturally tanned instead of burning like me. I envied her for that alone.

"Hey! Sorry, I'm late. I was trying to get Keela to come, but she is out cold at home. Poor thing is overworked."

She was talking about her best friend, Keela Daley.

Keela was a cool girl. I've met her a few times before, and I liked her. I just hated who she happened to be related to.

I grimaced as I thought of her cousin, Micah Daley that fucking bitch and her horrible boyfriend, Jason Bane, put me through hell during our school years.

"Bronagh!" Aideen shouted getting my attention.

I smiled and got up to give her a hug.

"Happy birthday!"

She put her arms around my body and hugged me tight. We when pulled apart I turned to the table and pointed to everyone.

"This is Do—"

"Nico," Dominic said as he cut me off, "and I'm her boyfriend."

Aideen nodded. "Nice to meet you, Nico."

I ignored Dominic's rudeness and looked at Alec and Kane. "That's Alec, and that's Kane. Dominic's brothers."

Alec winked at Aideen while Kane grinned and said, "Nice to meet you, gorgeous."

Aideen laughed. "You're right, it *is* nice to meet me."

Kane furrowed his eyebrows in confusion while I laughed. Aideen completely ignored Kane then and turned to Ryder when he broke away from his friends to greet her.

"Hey darling, you made it."

Aideen gave him a hug. "Hey Ry, I wouldn't miss it."

I smiled when "Work Bitch" by Britney Spears came on.

I *loved* this song.

I looked at Branna. "I wanna dance."

Branna nodded her head in Dominic's direction. "Don't annoy him by goin' back down to the dance floor. We can dance here, instead if you want."

I was game.

"You better work bitch!" I shouted making Branna laugh as we threw our hands up in the air and pumped our hips to the beat of the song.

Aideen quickly joined in our dancing. She had a drink in hand and took a sip every few seconds and shook her arse, which I found hilarious. I turned my back to the girls and danced over to Dominic, who was leaning back against the booth seat as he watched me.

He smirked when I held my hand out to him.

"I'm not dancing to a Britney Spears' song. Not a chance."

I frowned.

Dominic shook his head. "Stop it. I'm not doing what you want just because you frown."

Damn.

I turned around and continued to dance. I moved back every few seconds, cornering Dominic with my arse.

I jumped and swung around when he smacked it.

I rubbed the sting away.

"That hurt."

Dominic growled. "It was either I spank it or bite it."

I snapped my teeth at him, which Alec snickered over.

"Come on, get up and dance with me... it's me birthday."

I frowned.

Dominic groaned, and I knew I was so close to breaking him but the music I was dancing to suddenly stopped and the sound of drums could be heard.

Oh, no.

The fights were starting.

"Ladies and gents," a loud voice boomed throughout the Playhouse as I sat down on Dominic's lap.

"We have some great events lined up for you all tonight, if you'll make your way off the dance floor we will raise the platform."

I watched as security of the Playhouse ushered every person off the dance floor then stood back themselves. I leaned up so I could see the platform rise, I thought it looked cool and tried to watch it every time I was here for a fight.

It was a brilliant design. When the platform was lowered, it was a flat floor, but when it was raised up in the air, it stood a few feet off the ground, which was a bit of a drop when the fighters got knocked off it.

I leaned my head against Dominic's shoulder as he stroked my thigh with his thumb.

I was about to ask if he wanted a drink when the voice of the Playhouse announcer spoke,

"I've just got word that RAMPAGE is in the club!"

Oh, no.

Chapter Nine

"Nico... where you at, man? You can call the first fight."

Loads of people shouted and pointed over at our table. I closed my eyes when Dominic tapped my back and asked me to stand up off him.

I grabbed his arm when we both stood up. "You said you weren't fightin'."

Dominic looked down at me and said, "I'm not."

"Promise?"

He nodded but didn't say the words.

I let him go and watched as he walked down to the platform and hoisted himself up onto it. I sat down in Dominic's seat and folded my arms across my chest. I hated the attention he got during a fight—the crowd seemed to flood with pulsing vaginas that all wanted a piece of him.

Dominic pulled two fighters up on to the platform and spoke to them, gestured his hands at both of them and laughed. A second later both fighters attacked each other, and cheers filled the playhouse.

I clenched my jaw and fists when someone threw a piece of fabric at Dominic. He picked it up and laughed. It was a bra.

"You look mad, bee."

I nodded to Alec. "I am. They treat him like a celebrity."

Alec put his arm around my shoulder and said, "In this world he is a celebrity. Everyone loves an underground fighter, even if he doesn't go pro."

I swallowed.

Dominic got offers from different coaches and gyms to train with them to try and crack the UFC world. I didn't think I had ever been so relieved as when he told me he'd turned every offer down.

He loved fighting but only because it was a hobby and a stress reliever. He didn't have enough passion to pursue it as a career.

His passion was in fitness training.

He loved fitness and the human body, so after we had graduated from school, he went to college and got all his qualifications. He was a Personal Trainer, but not one who worked in a gym. He had a client list, his own website, and worked his arse off with each client every time he had a session.

I was damn proud of him for having a career and going to work happy every day, while I was at home bored because I didn't know what to do with myself. I wasn't lazy—I just didn't have a dream job like everyone else. I was more than happy to be a stay at home mother... the problem was we didn't have any children.

Yet.

"Hey, you okay?"

I jumped like I was caught doing something wrong.

I swallowed and looked at Alec. "Yeah."

Alec raised his eyebrows. "What were you thinking about just then?"

I shrugged.

"Tell me."

I sighed.

"Don't repeat this to Dominic."

Alec nodded. "I won't say a word."

I smiled. "I was thinking about how happy I am that Dominic has his personal trainer job, but then it got me thinkin' about what job I'll end up doin' for the rest of me life and then it dawned on me that the only job I want to do is be a stay at home ma."

Alec stared at me then looked down to my stomach and back up to my face.

"Are you *pregnant*?" he asked, his eyes wide.

I laughed. "No... But I think I'm ready to be."

It made my pulse spike saying that out loud. I've thought of motherhood loads of times over the past few weeks but saying it out loud made it seem like it could actually be a possibility, instead of *just* a thought.

"Bronagh!?"

Alec was wide-eyed, and I couldn't blame him. There was no warning for this big news—it was just a little thought that developed into something I wanted for Dominic and myself. I never even hinted about children, but lately when I was on my own it was all I thought about.

I chuckled. "I know we're only twenty-one, and we aren't married, but since when does any of that matter?"

Alec was shocked.

Very shocked.

"I didn't even think you liked kids."

I shrugged my shoulders. "I like kids. But it's only in these past few weeks that I've been thinkin' about how brilliant it would be for me and Dominic to have a baby of our own... I am home on me own a lot so I've thought about this. I've just never said anythin' because I didn't want to make things weird."

Alec scratched his head. "Wow."

I nodded my head. "Yeah, wow."

I was surprised when Alec kissed my head then and said, "Tell him."

Excuse me?

I shook my head. "No way, I'll terrify him."

Alec frowned. "I think it might scare him a little bit but the prospect of fatherhood does that to all men. Dominic he loves you, bee. He wants a family with you. I don't think there will ever be a right time to plan one, either, and life is short, so I say go for it."

Oh, my goodness.

"You're not helpin' me kick this sudden obsession, you know?"

Alec laughed. "I'd like to have a niece or nephew, so I'm in your corner."

I looked down. "Dominic might not be."

Alec snapped his fingers. "If he doesn't want a baby, you can trap him, just stop taking your pill. I'll even poke holes in the condoms if you use them."

"Alec, I'm not trappin' Dominic with a baby!"

Alec burst out laughing. "I was only playing... but now that I think about it, you should tell him you're pregnant just to see his reaction. If he is happy, you can break the news you aren't pregnant, but then you can both start trying for a baby, and if he cries, you can tell him it was a joke and give him a few years to grow into his daddy shoes."

If only it were that easy.

I laughed. "What would I say? Hey Dominic, guess what? I'm pregnant with your baby. *Surprise.*"

Alec opened his mouth to speak, but his jaw dropped open as he looked over my head.

"You're *pregnant*?!"

Oh, fuck.

I snapped in Dominic's direction, and I was so shocked that I could do nothing but stare at him.

The fight was over that fucking fast?

I moved my mouth, but no sounds came out. Dominic dropped to his knees in front of me and looked down at my stomach then back up at me.

Oh God, he thinks I'm pregnant!

"I can't believe this... Are you having a baby? *My* baby?"

He looked.... pleased?

"No," I said and watched as Dominic sat back and looked at me with confused eyes. "I'm not pregnant, Dominic."

His frown deepened. "I heard what you said to Alec. You were practicing how to tell me. I *heard* you."

I shook my head and then glanced to everyone else. My sister, Aideen, Ryder, his friends, Kane and more people who were looking at us with wide eyes.

Oh, my God!

"I'm *not* pregnant!" I snapped.

I looked back at Dominic. "You overheard a joke."

Dominic's jaw set. "A joke? Why would you joke about something like that? I don't find it one fucking bit funny."

I swallowed.

"Rip it off like a Band-Aid and tell him," Alec murmured from behind me.

"Oh, God," I mumbled.

Dominic put his hands on my face and forced me to look at him. "What's going on, Bronagh? You can tell me."

Quick and painless.

"This is sudden and completely out of the blue. I *know* it's goin' to sound absolutely crazy because we're only twenty-one but... I want us to have a baby," I said very fast then closed my eyes.

Silence.

Utter fucking silence.

Oh, Christ. Dominic is going to break up with me. I have scared the love of my life away with the B word!

"I take it back, it's fine. I don't want any children—"

I was cut off when I felt Dominic's lips briefly touch mine. I blinked when I looked at him and found him staring back at me.

"How long have you been thinking about this?" he asked.

I swallowed.

He didn't sound mad or look scared.

I shrugged my shoulders. "I can't really pinpoint when the

thought developed, but it's been on me mind awhile. I just want us to expand our family... maybe I'm bein' stupid, I don't know."

Dominic pecked my lips. "You're not stupid for wanting us to start a family, pretty girl."

I'm not?

"I'm not?" I murmured.

Dominic shook his head. "No, we'll be together three years next month, maybe it's normal for thoughts of us having a kid together to start."

He was taking this surprisingly well.

"I think it's different for everyone. Some people think about kids after a few years, some after a few decades. I don't know, but the thought of us having a baby just gives me butterflies."

Dominic let his eyes roam over my face.

"Okay," he said.

Okay.

Okay what?

"I'm sorry, what was that?"

Dominic laughed. "I said okay. We can have a baby."

I stared at him.

"Fuck off, you're pullin' me leg."

Dominic burst out laughing and shook his head. "No, I'm serious. Let's have a baby."

My mouth went dry.

"But you said we weren't getting married until we were older."

"Yes, we can get married at any time, but you want a baby now—and I want a baby now."

What. The. Fuck?

"Are you jokin'?" I asked.

"No, I'm serious."

I don't believe him.

"I don't believe you."

Dominic laughed. "Okay, I'll flush all your birth control pills when we get home to prove I'm telling you the truth."

Oh, my God.

"You *want* a baby?" I asked.

He chewed on his lower lip. "I never thought of it to be honest, but when I heard you say you were pregnant it made me happy. Very happy. I now have a picture in my mind of your belly swollen with my baby and I love it."

I felt tears gather at the corner of my eyes.

"Okay, we're tryin' then?" I asked.

He nodded. "Yep, we're trying to get knocked up."

I burst out laughing and kissed him.

When we broke apart and I turned to everyone who was looking at us like they have no idea what was happening.

"We decided we're goin' to try and get pregnant." I beamed.

Branna blinked.

"What?"

I smiled. "I know it's sudden… but it feels right for us."

"Shut the front door!" Aideen squealed just as Branna rushed at Dominic and me and hugged us both to her.

"I can't believe this!" she cried.

I laughed and comforted her.

"Yeah! Hugs all around for Dominic and Bronagh announcing they are going to fuck like rabbits to try and conceive a child! Wa-hoo!"

Dominic, his brothers, and anyone who heard Alec doubled over laughing.

"How long does it take for her to get pregnant after she stops taking her pills?" Dominic asked Branna when everyone started up conversations with one another.

Branna wiped her face and smiled. "It can happen after a month or as long as a year. There is no set timeframe. It is different for every woman's body... but the more the sex, the better chances."

Dominic punched the air. "More sex. Yes."

I looked at him. "We have sex all the time."

He smirked. "I know, but now we have a better reason to do it all the time."

I smiled and hugged him.

We are trying to get pregnant.

Holy fuck!

That was *not* how I expected my night to go.

I danced around with everyone then for a while and ignored all the fights going on behind us on the platform. I cheered Aideen on when she knocked back two shots and then I sat her next to Kane when she declared she wanted to kiss him.

"She wants to kiss you!" I shouted to Kane.

Kane turned to Aideen, and he was about to open his mouth and speak when Aideen suddenly launched herself at him.

"Oh, fuck... her arse in showin'!" I shouted to Kane.

He adjusted Aideen on top of his body then reached around and pulled her dress down and held it down by keeping his hands firmly on her arse.

"Should we stop her?" I shouted to Branna. "She isn't drunk, but she is well on her way."

Branna came beside me. "Do you really want to be the person stoppin' *that* possible one-night stand from happenin'? Besides, I think you might lose a finger if you try and separate them."

I looked at Kane and Aideen, who were sloppy kissing and grinding against one another. Branna was right—there was no way I was breaking those two up.

"Leave them be."

Branna laughed at me.

I glanced around us for the lads.

"Where are Dominic and Ryder?"

"Gone to the bar with some friends. They said they wouldn't be long," Branna shouted over the music.

I nodded my head. "Just goin' the bathroom. I've to pass the bar, so I'll give him a shout as I go by."

Branna nodded her head, so I walked down through the crowds in the direction of the bar. I leaned up trying to spot Dominic or his brothers and did so with a spring to my step. I was going to check in with Dominic and then go to the bathroom. I walked over to them, but I was knocked back when a man bumped into me.

He laughed when he seen me stumble, and that annoyed me.

"Excuse *you*!" I snapped.

He looked surprised that I shouted at him.

"*You* walked into *me*."

"Yes, and I was goin' to apologise until you laughed."

The man only grinned at me. "It was funny watchin' you try to stay on your feet."

Fucking dickhead.

"Prick," I said to myself then started forward.

I shouted when the man grabbed my arm and pulled me against him. "What did you call me? A prick? Who do you think you're talkin' to, you ugly little cunt?"

I tried to pull myself free, but the man had a firm grip on my arm.

"Dominic!" I screamed.

I knew he was at the bar in front of me so I screamed as loud as I could. The man holding me ducked his head and shook me.

"Shut the fuck up screechin'!"

"Bronagh?" I heard Dominic call.

"Dominic!"

"Get the fuck away from her!"

I was shoved backwards when Dominic tackled the man who was hurting me. Two lads caught me from falling. I thanked them and looked back just in time to see Dominic rise to his feet. The man he tackled got up as well.

"Let me guess, the ugly cunt is your bitch?"

Dominic swung with his right arm and caught the man with a perfectly timed right hook across the jaw. The man's head snapped to the side and he dropped to the ground like a sack of potatoes.

I flung my hands over my mouth when he didn't get up.

"Fuck. He knocked him out with *one* dig!"

I ignored the shouts from the lads behind me and moved to Dominic's side. "Are you okay?" I asked.

"Am I okay? Are *you* okay?"

I nodded. "I'm fine. His bark was worse than his bite."

Dominic was pissed as he took my hand and led me away. I tugged him in the direction of the bathroom because I still had to go.

"Can you stay put, Bronagh?" Dominic asked as he followed me into the girl's toilets.

"Get out, this is the ladies."

Dominic didn't say anything, he only held onto the sinks to steady himself.

"Are you drunk?" I asked.

He wiggled his fingers. "Just a little buzzed. I haven't drunk alcohol in a long time."

I frowned. "So, why drink tonight?"

"I wasn't planning on it, but then we decided to try for a baby so I figured what the fuck, let's celebrate."

I snorted as I went into a bathroom stall, pulled down my booty shorts and suspenders and relieved myself.

"Are you still there?" I asked.

"Yes."

I shook my head and grabbed some tissue, wiped myself then stood up and flushed the toilet.

"Where were you going before that guy grabbed you?" Dominic asked me when I exited the stall and moved to the sinks to wash my hands.

"To see where you were."

"Why?"

I shrugged. "Just wanted to see where you were."

Why so curious?

"Why?" I asked.

Dominic shrugged. "Wanted to know what you followed me for."

I frowned. "I didn't follow you, I was just checking in to see—"

"Checking in? Jesus, Bronagh, I'm not a kid. You don't have to check in on me."

What?

"No, that's not what I meant—"

"I mean I was away from you for two minutes. Did you think I ran away or something?"

Where in the hell is all this comin' from?

"What the fuck is with you? Why are you pickin' a fight with me for?" I bellowed.

Dominic shrugged. "Not picking a fight, just saying it like it is."

"You're makin' it out like I'm clingy with you."

Dominic laughed. "You *are* clingy with me, baby."

Excuse me?

"No, I'm fuckin' not."

"Yeah, you are."

Oh, my God.

"Because I wanted to see where you were at means I'm clingy? Okay, then yeah, I'm *so* clingy. What I want to know is why do you act like that bothers you?"

Dominic blinked. "Because I like some freedom to chill with my brothers and friends without my woman's head up my ass twenty-four-seven."

What. The. Fuck?

"You're bang out of fuckin' line here. If you have something you want to say to me, fuckin' say it."

Dominic was silent, but I could tell he wanted to talk. He just didn't know how to word it.

I swallowed. "If I'm so clingy and it bothers you so much then why did you agree to us tryin' for a baby?"

"Because I *want* a baby with you... I'd just like you to—"

"Take me head out of your arse?"

Dominic laughed. "You said it pretty girl, not me."

I was hurt, and I was furious.

"The only thing up your arse will be me foot, you dickhead!" I snapped.

"Oh, here comes the dramatics. I was waiting for them to kick in."

I stared at him. "I'm sick of this."

"Sick of *what*?"

"This. Us fightin' all the bloody time."

Dominic groaned. "We fight all the time because you turn every argument into a fight—Not now, use the men's room!"

I looked at the girl Dominic snapped at and watched her flee back out the restroom door. Dominic turned his head back to me, and he didn't look so buzzed anymore.

"We fight because you can't just converse when things get tough. You have to freak out."

I felt my heart pound.

How the hell did we go from being on a baby-trying-high to a situation so sour, all in the space of half an hour?

"I can't do this anymore, Dominic. I'm not fuckin' tall enough to ride your emotional rollercoaster!"

"So, get on your tip toes," he snarled. "Because it's one ride you're never getting off. I'm your fucking life, not just your boyfriend. We need each other, don't you get that? We *need* each other."

I blinked.

"This is why I get mad at you, Bronagh. If I say something stupid or react wrongly, you don't give me enough time to realise that I'm being a dick, you just go crazy. I shouldn't have said what I just did about you being clingy, but you went off on me before I even got the chance to think of apologising."

I folded my arms. "You want to apologise for bein' a dick?"

He snorted. "Not anymore because your lovely attitude has made me rethink saying sorry."

Oh, he is full of it.

I rolled my eyes and Dominic narrowed his.

"Why must everything be over the top with you, Bronagh? I try to tell you that I want just a little space so I can hang out with my brothers and friends and you get defensive. I said it the wrong way—I know that—but you reacted in typical Bronagh style just as I should have expected."

"Typical Bronagh style, what is that exactly?"

"It's you acting like a damn child."

What the hell?

"I don't act like—"

"Yeah, Bronagh, you do. You're immature."

I was immature?

"That's rich comin' from you."

Dominic sighed. "I'm aware of when I'm being immature, but you aren't."

I blinked.

"Why are you being like this?"

Dominic shrugged. "I'm not being like anything. This is just me finally saying something about the reaction I get from you all the time when things go south. You think we're ready for big things, and I want that to be true, but you have the attitude of a teenager when you get mad."

Wow.

"Tell me how you really feel."

Dominic looked at me. "I love you more that life itself, I swear on my life that I do. I *want* to have a child with you. I want to be with you forever... but you need to grow up *with* me. That's what I'm trying to say here. I've been thinking of a way to say this to you for the past year and I haven't come up with a way to say it without thinking you will break up with me in a temper tantrum. We aren't in high school anymore, Bronagh. The tantrums have to *stop* at some stage."

I swallowed.

"I'm not tryin' to hurt you, baby, but I think you might have some sort of anger problem. I have a temper that is spiked easily, but damn when I say one thing to you, you explode verbally or physically. I walk on eggshells around you most days because I don't know what you will do. I admit I react wrong by laughing at you or playing everything off as a joke, but I don't know what else to do to take the tension out of the situation. Do you understand that? I just don't know."

I felt my stomach drop.

"Why does this feel like a break up?" I whispered.

Dominic sighed. "No one is breaking up, we're in this for the long haul. But I need to know if you're in my corner fighting for me, or if you in the opposing corner fighting against me. It's easier to fight when we're fighting for the same thing, pretty girl."

I looked down.

"Yeah, what's that?"

"Our relationship."

My head was swimming, and I couldn't think.

Our relationship needs fighting for?

"Why have you never mentioned this before? I had no idea you thought we were in trouble."

Dominic sighed. "I'm sorry, I know it's sudden but just like you've been thinking about having a baby, I've been thinking about how we need to change. Our relationship isn't the healthiest, baby. We are in no way a normal couple, but we shouldn't fight as much as we do over stupid things. You're a smart girl, I know you would have thought of this sooner or later."

I remained silent.

"I am so sorry for pulling a three-sixty and springing this on you on your birthday, but if we're going to do big things together, I think we need to be on the same page. I felt like I had to get this off my chest instead of sitting next to you and smiling like I haven't been thinking about these things."

I sniffled.

"I hate that this upsets you. I want to protect you from everything."

I sniffled. "And who protects you if you protect me all the time?"

Dominic smiled. "Once you're in my corner and you're really *with* me, that's all the protection I need, pretty girl."

I closed my eyes.

"Do you hate me?" he asked.

Stupid question.

"I don't see a day where I will feel anythin' close to hate when it comes to you."

Silence.

"I've tried to give you subtle hints over the last few months. I've told you to grow up or act your age hoping it would click in your head that your behaviour can be… out there."

My stomach hurt, and a lump formed in my throat.

"Look, I'm going to do something I've never done before. I'm going to let you *think* about everything I just said instead of turning this into make-up sex, okay? I'll go back to our table. Come back when you're ready."

I was shocked when I opened my eyes and looked up only to find Dominic was gone.

He was serious about everything he said but what the hell brought it on?

He had never mentioned my anger in a serious discussion before, nor had he ever said I needed to fight *with* him instead of *against* him.

He said he had thought about getting it off his chest for a while, but what the hell triggered him to lay this all out tonight?

He said what he did because he thinks we're ready for the big thing.

What big thing?

I thought on it for a minute then gasped.

"The baby talk," I murmured aloud.

Oh, my god.

When I sprung that I wanted us to have a baby, it must have brought this up in his mind. A baby was serious. He knew we're serious, but having a baby made us *really* serious.

"He wants us to be strong together so we don't fall apart if we have a baby."

I went into a bathroom stall, closed the door and then sat down on the closed toilet lid and cried.

I didn't know we were in trouble.

How could I have been so blind?

Am I ruining us?

Am I the reason we fight all the time?

Do... Do I have an anger problem?

I calmed myself down so I could think clearly.

I knew straight off the bat that Dominic really *was* my life and that I needed him because, without him, I wasn't me. Nothing would make sense without him. I wanted a family with him. Despite our arguments, I knew we were ready for a baby, but to make us a *happy* family, Dominic was right. I needed put a stamp on my temper and my knee-jerk reaction to things... I needed help.

I needed to talk to Branna.

She was a mid-wife. She must know of some classes or something that help people deal with anger and emotions.

I nodded my head, stood up, and exited the toilet stall. I made the decision to fight in Dominic's corner and to fight for us *with* him. I would protect him like him did me.

I looked around the restroom and shook my head.

I thought life-changing decisions were meant to be made in the shower?

Chapter Ten

I exited the bathroom, but I didn't want to walk the way I came, in case the fella Dominic knocked out was awake, so I walked around the opposite side of the platform. I stayed close to the platform because most people hung back so they could watch any fights. It made getting by easier.

I was walking along fine until I felt a tap on my head.

I looked up.

"Hey," a redhead girl shouted down from the platform. "Can you help me off this thing? Some of the lads pushed me up as a joke."

Men.

"Sure, I could catch you—"

"Could you give me your hand?"

Uh.

"Okay," I said and reached my arm up and placed my hand in hers. "But I don't see how that will—Omigod."

Hands grabbed onto the back of my thighs and pushed me up into the air. The girl who had my arm pulled me until I stumbled onto the platform.

"What the fuck was that?!" I snapped and carefully got to my feet.

I looked at the girl who was in shorts, a sports bra and hand wraps around her hands.

Oh, no.

She was a fighter.

"You're fightin' me tonight."

I heard her wrong.

"I beg your pardon?"

"You. Are. Fightin'. Me. Tonight."

Okay, I heard her clearly this time, but I was *not* in the mood for jokes.

"Listen, what's your name?"

"Jennifer."

"Listen, *Jennifer*, I've a lot goin' on right now. Can we please cut the bullshit here?"

Jennifer laughed. "The only bullshit is that you think you can go around startin' shite and cause people to get hurt."

What?

"I have *no* idea what you're talkin' about—"

"Ladies, and gents. Who's ready for a CATFIGHT?"

Does that mean Jennifer and me?

The screams and shouts were deafening.

"I'm not!" I shouted. "I'm not ready... I'm in heels and a fucking dress!"

I screamed and jumped to the side when Jennifer suddenly came at me.

This is not fucking happening.

"Oh, please! I don't want to fight you!"

I was crying, but can you blame me? This bitch wanted to kick my arse.

"Why me?" I asked as tears fell down my cheeks.

"Because *your* fella knocked *mine* fuckin' out."

Wait, the lad who hurt me and called me ugly was her fella?
"That dickhead is your fella?"
Jennifer growled.
I panicked. "I take it back, he isn't a dickhead. Don't kill me!"
Jennifer took a step forward.
I took a step back.
"Can we not just talk about this? I'll buy you a pint!"
Jennifer shook her head. "No, you're on the platform, so let's just do this."
"But I'm a beacon for peace. I wouldn't hurt a fly!"
She didn't know me, so she didn't know how much of a lie that was.
"Tough shit, princess."
Princess!
I turned and tried to escape, I was going to run and jump off the platform but there was somehow a fucking cage around the platform now.
A cage.
I have never seen a cage around the platform.
Never.
"What the fuck is this?" I screamed and looked around.
Where the fuck did the cage come from?
"They lower it down on the second Friday of every month."
Oh.
That was nice.
I ran up to the nice cage, reached out and shook it with all my fucking might.
"Dominic!" I screamed.
I searched the crowd for him, his brothers, and my sister, but all I could see were drunk faces dancing to the pulsing music.
"Bronagh, watch out!"
I swung around when I heard Dominic's voice, then screamed when I looked at Jennifer and realised she was coming at me. Literally.

Why does the most random shite happen to me?

I dove to the left and quickly scrambled back to my feet in time to watch Jennifer run into the cage. Usually, I would call that person stupid, but I was happy because I was hoping it would knock her out.

Not with my luck though, because she got back up and was angrier than before.

"Oh, Jesus... Oh, Christ."

I am going to die.

"Babe, listen to me, okay? Put your hands up in front of your face."

I nodded my head and covered my face.

"No! *Guard* your face, Bronagh, don't fuckin' cover it!"

I dropped my hands and held them out in front of my face.

"How the hell am I supposed to know what to do? I've never done this before?" I bellowed at Dominic.

I wished I knew where he was because when he spoke, it sounded like he was all around me.

"Is this a lover's tiff?" Jennifer asked as she danced around the ring while I stood still in the centre of it.

"No, this is normal for us. So normal that you would think we need a shrink... I'm actually considerin' goin' to anger manage— Ahhhh!"

I kicked my legs out at Jennifer when she was close. I meant to kick her, but my heels flew off and hit her in the chest and head by mistake.

The heel to the head hurt her though because she grabbed her head and fell backwards.

I screamed then ran to the side of the cage. "Someone get me out of here, this is a mistake! I'm a lover, *not* a fighter!"

"Move left! Left, left, left!" Dominic's voice shouted.

I swung left. "She isn't on me left!"

"Your other fucking left!"

I swung to my right and instantly threw my hands up in front of my face. I felt a punch hit me in the side of the head and seconds later I felt my body hit the ground.

"Lift the fucking cage!" I heard numerous voices shout.

I was dizzy and felt like I was going to be sick.

I tried to sit up, but I received another whack to my face then I felt a weight on my chest pinning me down. I opened my eyes and found Jennifer sat on top of me. I closed my eyes, covered my head with my hands, and cringed.

I was pretty sure I screamed when she began raining punches to my head, but it didn't last long because one second she was on me, then the next she wasn't.

I opened my eyes and turned to the right in time to see Dominic pin Jennifer to the ground and shout down into her face. Security guards got up onto the platform and took hold of Jennifer so Dominic could move over to me.

"Jesus, baby," he said, he eyes wide as he looked down at me.

I winced. "I'm fine. Sore, but fine... I thought I was gonna die."

Dominic pressed his hand to my cheek and it hurt.

"What the hell happened? *Why* did you get up here—"

"I didn't," I cut him off. "She tricked me. It was her fella who you knocked out at the bar... She must have seen the whole thing from up here. She wanted revenge on me."

"Fuck's sake," Dominic growled.

I reached up and touched his face and then out of the corner of my eye I saw Jennifer break out of the security guard's hold and rush at Dominic.

I found the strength to pull myself up and pulled him to the other side of me. I didn't know what I planned to do to Jennifer when she got to me, but I luckily didn't have to worry because the security guards caught her and pulled her back.

"Bronagh, what the fuck are you doing?"

I looked at Dominic and shrugged. "What does it look like I'm doin'? I'm protectin' you."

Dominic blinked, his eyes softening. "Baby."

I leaned my head against his. "I thought about what you said, and you are right. You were right about *everythin'*. I'm sorry I've never seen the underlyin' issue with us. I promise that I'm goin' to find a class or a course to help me deal with me emotions in the correct way. I'm in your corner with you for life. I love you."

Dominic swallowed. "I love you so fucking much."

He kissed my mouth, but it was too rough so I pulled back and hissed.

"I don't mean to ruin the moment, but I feel like I'm dyin'. Can you get me off this thing?"

"Of course," Dominic said.

After a few minutes, we were back at our table. I sat down across from Aideen and Alec, and groaned.

"Can we go home?" I asked.

"We're leaving now bumble be—"

"Alec."

I jumped at the loud female screech.

"Yes?" Alec asked the blonde haired girl.

"Who is that bitch? Tonight's shag?" she snapped.

Alec looked down to Aideen, who was half asleep on his shoulder and laughed. It looked like he was about to say something, but he was cut off when the girl suddenly attacked Aideen.

"What the fuck?" I screamed.

Kane jumped over the table and pulled the girl off Aideen, who was holding onto her cheek.

"Get the fuck out of here!" Kane snarled to the bitch he was holding and shoved her away from our table.

She left but cursed every one of us along the way.

"Aideen?" I called.

She whimpered.

"Fuck!" Kane snapped.

I frowned.

What the fuck is with all the fighting tonight?

"I want to go home," Aideen sniffled.

"I'll bring you—"

"No, I want Keela. Ring Keela!"

Kane and Alec shared a look.

Alec sighed. "Give me your phone and I'll ring her."

Aideen gave Alec her phone then went with Kane as he helped her leave. I frowned as they walked away.

Poor Aideen.

I winced then when my cheek throbbed.

Poor me.

"Ryder and Branna are waiting for us, Bronagh—Wait, where are Aideen and Kane?"

I shrugged. "Some girl attacked Aideen."

"What? Why?"

I opened my mouth to answer Dominic, but I didn't know who or why the girl attacked Aideen.

"Alec, why did that girl address you before she jumped on Aideen?"

Alec scratched his head. "I think I fucked her and her boyfriend last week."

I deadpanned.

He was such a slut.

Dominic shook his head and helped me up. "Are you ready to go home, baby?"

I nodded my head. "We've been out for hours. I need to check on Tyson."

"We fed him and let him go the bathroom before we left. He is fine."

"He is a puppy."

Dominic groaned. "Okay fine, let's go and check on your baby."

I smiled and kissed his cheek. "I love you."

"And I love you."

"Do you love me?"

I looked at Alec and grinned. "Oh, yeah."

Dominic chuckled. "Are you leaving with us?"

Alec shook his head and stood up. "I've got to go help Kane

with Branna's friend. I have to ring..."

"Keela," I provided.

Alec nodded. "Yeah, I have to ring Keela."

"Be nice to her. It's the early hours and you will be wakin' her up."

Alec laughed. "I'm ringing a girl to come pick up her friend, I've got this."

He turned and walked off.

Dominic frowned. "Maybe I should go call Keela instead of him."

I shook my head and squeezed Dominic's hand.

"Nah, let him do it. You never know, it could be the start of somethin' beautiful."

ALEC
a slater brothers novella

CHAPTER ONE

"Miss Daley? Open up! I know you're in there, your car is outside in the tenant car park!"

I groaned at the sound of the loud voice, and flicked my eyes open then quickly re-closed them. It took a few moments for me to be able to keep them open, and when I could, I couldn't see very well. I squinted through the darkness waiting for my eyes to adjust to the minimal lighting. When I could finally see, I quickly narrowed my eyes at the fat snoring male beside me. I shoved him hoping to knock him off the bed, but instead of falling off like I'd hoped he only farted and rolled over in my direction then placed a big sloppy kiss on my mouth.

"Storm!" I shouted and wiped at my mouth and tried not to

heave, but the smell of Storm's breath made that very hard.

Storm lazily got to his feet, stretched and made some weird noises then proceeded to belly flop on top of me until I gasped for air. Storm, my two year old German Shepherd, needed to be put on a diet or one of these days the fat baby was going to smother me in my sleep.

"Off!" I gasped and shoved at his large body with both of my hands.

Storm did as ordered and got off me. But he didn't get off the bed, instead he just rolled back over to his side—yes, my dog had a side of the bed—which was just typical. The only time he willingly moved was if it was breakfast time, lunch time, dinner time or pretty much any time he knew there would be food in it for him.

"You pathetic excuse for a guard dog," I muttered as the banging on my apartment door started up again.

Storm replied with another fart that had me opening the windows before I left my bedroom to proceed down the hallway to open my door. I stubbed my toe on one of Storm's doggy toys as I walked and cursed the person on the other side of the door for making me get out of bed—it was the middle of the night for God's sake!

"I'm comin', keep your knickers on!" I shouted when I reached my door and began unlocking all the locks. There were five of them in total because in the area where I lived, one lock was not enough. I switched on my hall light and jumped when the bulb blew, coating the hall in darkness once again. I sighed as I turned to my front door, even though I was pretty sure I knew who was on the other side, I still looked through the peephole just to be safe.

When I confirmed the noisy menace at my door was in fact my neighbour, I unlocked the final lock and pulled it open then harshly glared at the man who was stood before me. Mr. Pervert—his real name was Mr. Doyle—was a middle-aged man who was the CEO at Perverts 'R Us. The man was a major creep, and I hated that I answered the door to him dressed in nothing but my nightdress because it gave him free rein to ogle me with his ever-roaming eyes.

"Can I help you, Mr. Per-Doyle?" I asked, biting my tongue so I didn't laugh at almost calling him Mr. Pervert out loud.

He snapped his eyes up from gawking at my legs to my face and cleared his throat as he lifted his hand—a hand that contained one single envelope. I simply stared at the envelope for a moment then flicked my eyes up to Mr. Pervert and found his eyes weren't on my face anymore. I knocked on the outside of my door with my free hand which made him jump with fright and me inwardly snort. When his eyes were once again on mine, I nodded to the envelope in his hand and then raised my brows in a silent question.

He cleared his throat again before he said, "I've been away the last few weeks and found this in my mailbox when I got home a few moments ago. It is addressed to you, but has my apartment number on it instead of yours."

I wanted to punch him. I used the light from the hallway outside of my apartment to look back inside and lock my eyes on the clock hanging on the wall behind me, it was twenty past three in the morning.

Couldn't he have just waited till morning before he delivered it to me?

The bloody eejit!

I sighed as I turned back to Mr. Pervert, who was back to looking at my body. I reached out and gripped the envelope and gave it a little tug until Mr. Pervert released it.

"Thanks, I appreciate you goin' out of your way to make sure I get me post." I faked a smile and then pulled the hand that now held the envelope away until it was tucked safely behind my door—along with the rest of my body—so Mr. Pervert couldn't see me anymore.

He blinked a few times and looked at my face, because it was now all that he could see.

"It was no problem at all, sweetheart."

Sweetheart? No!

I smiled and nodded my head as I inched my door closed. "Good night."

"Good—" I closed the door before he could finish his sentence.

I shook off my shivers then I relocked all of the locks on and closed the bolt at the top of the door. I breathed a sigh of relief when I heard Mr. Pervert's footsteps trot back across the hall and into his own apartment where he closed the door behind him. I looked at the envelope in my hand and decided to open it because I was curious as to what was inside it. I couldn't see very well because the hallway was still dark but I knew it wasn't a bill, it didn't feel like the envelope bills came in, it was thicker. From what I had seen it looked nicer than a bill envelope. Fancier.

I headed into my kitchen that also doubled as my sitting room and flicked on the light. I tossed the envelope on the kitchen table and went to the counter drawers to look for my envelope cutter. I found it after only a second of looking, but had to put it down when I heard my phone ring from my bedroom. I furrowed my eyebrows in confusion.

Who the hell would be calling me at twenty past three in the morning?

"Aideen," I said out loud and headed in the direction of my bedroom.

Aideen Collins was my best friend. She was the closest thing I had to a sister and I loved her dearly, but she had her moments when she royally pissed me off. Ringing me at half past three in the morning was one of those moments.

When I got to the phone in my bedroom and pressed answer I said, "You'd better have a good reason for ringin' me at this hour Aideen Collins or I am goin' to kick seven shades of shite outta you!"

I heard a deep, rumbling chuckle.

"She *does* have a good reason, so you don't need to kick any shade of shit out of her," a male voice replied, it made me jump with fright because I wasn't expecting it.

"Who are you? Where is Aideen? Why do you have her phone?" I asked then gasped and shouted, "If you have hurt me friend in any way I'm goin' to fuck you up!"

The stranger laughed this time and said, "Is that a promise, kitten?"

Ex-fucking-cuse me?

"Where is Aideen? You better tell me right now or I'm gonna—"

"Fuck me up? Yeah, I got that part," he chuckled again then before he could say anything else I heard a different male voice speak, "I asked you to ring the girl's friend, Alec. What the hell is taking so long?"

I mentally made a note of the name Alec in case I had to call the Guards.

"I'm talking to her friend, but I haven't been able to tell her the point of my call. She is too busy threatening to 'fuck me up' if I have hurt the girl," the lad who called me laughed.

I was mad and also scared as to where Aideen was and who these foreign guys were. I knew they weren't Irish or even English—their accents sounded too different—but I couldn't pinpoint where they were from because there was a lot of background noise. It sounded like music.

"Just tell her what I told you to say so she can get here already," the second lad said to the one who called me.

The lad who called me sighed and said, "Keela, I'm calling to let you know your friend Aiden was in a fight and we need you to come pick her up. She told me to call you."

"Her name is Aideen not Aiden, it's pronounced Ay-deen," I said then widened my eyes when I comprehended the rest of what he had just told me. I screamed, "Is she okay? What happened? Who hurt her?"

"Calm down, hellcat. She is fine, we just need you to come and collect her. I'll explain everything once you get here."

"Where is 'here'?" I snapped as I moved around my room pulling on my shoes. I grabbed my car keys from my bedside table as I held my phone to my ear with my shoulder.

"Playhouse Nightclub, it's right beside the Tallaght bypass—"

"I know where it is, I'll be there in five minutes," I said and hung up on him.

I gripped my phone and car keys in my hand as I closed my bedroom window. I told Storm to stay put, but it feel on deaf ears because he didn't move an inch or even wake up. I ran down my hallway and unlocked the locks and the bolt on my door then flung it open and sprung into the corridor. I closed my front door, locked it, then ran like a bat out of Hell down the hallway, down four flights of stairs and out into my apartment complex's car park. I sprinted towards my car and only realised I was in my nightdress when a cool breeze hit me and made me shiver.

"Fuck!" I snapped as I unlocked my car, got into it and started the engine.

I didn't think of changing my clothes, I just thought about getting my shoes on and then getting out to my car. I wasn't going back inside to change. I had to get to Aideen and make sure she was okay before changing clothes even became an option. It was okay though, I didn't show off any valuables. The nightdress was just a little short, it was black so I didn't have to worry that it was see through, at least I got lucky with that. The weather was good tonight as well, it was cool but not windy or raining. I would just have to hold the hem of my nightdress down when I got out of my car to keep it from rising up in case I had to run anywhere.

I pulled out of the car park and straight onto the main road and headed towards the nightclub. I was wide awake now, but the stinging in my eyes didn't go amiss. I had only been asleep for four hours before Mr. Pervert woke me up. Before that I hadn't slept in twenty-seven hours. I worked in my local supermarket, Super Value. I was broke and I needed all the hours I could get, so yesterday I worked an eleven hour shift and instead of going straight to bed when I got home, I dove straight into writing and pulled an all-nighter.

I have always had a passion for bringing the stories in my head to life on paper—or on a laptop screen. I only ever dabbled in silly little things here and there, never a full length novel. Luckily for me Aideen—literally—gave me the kick up the arse I needed and said I should just 'go for it' because I wouldn't know if my writing would be a success if I never put it out there. After my wake up call, which was three weeks ago, I knuckled down and started writing my very first book. Yesterday, even though I was shattered, I was completely in the zone and I just had to write. I had so much inside me for my story that if I didn't get it out of my head soon I was going to explode. So I wrote, wrote, and wrote some more. The lack of sleep and the stinging in my eyes from staring at my laptop was kicking my arse now though because I felt like death and I was pretty sure I looked the part too.

When I came to a red traffic light I pulled down my visor and looked in the little mirror and winced. Scratch that, saying I looked like death would have been kind. The sclera around my green eyes looked like a road map to Hell, that's how bloodshot they were. My fiery red hair was slightly greasy, and pulled up into a disastrous looking bun. I glanced down at my long bare white legs and shook my head.

Why did I have to be so tall?

If I were shorter, this nightdress would be longer and less exposing!

I angrily pushed my visor up when the traffic light changed to green and sped to the location of the nightclub Aideen was at with these men. I got there in less than five minutes because the green lights were with me, and there was little to no traffic on the roads thanks to the early hour. I turned into the nightclub car park entrance and looped around until I saw two huge males looking down at a small woman sitting down on the path a few meters away from the nightclub's entrance. It was Aideen, I just knew it. I parked my car across from them, jumped out, and slammed my door before I took off running towards Aideen.

When the sound of my feet hitting the pavement could be heard both men looked up at me, but didn't say anything as I reached them.

Once I was next to them, I dropped down to my knees and pulled Aideen into a hug. I ignored the slight stinging in my knees from the concrete ground digging into my skin and held Aideen tightly.

"Are you okay? What happened?" I asked then pulled back from the hug so I could look at her.

Aideen looked back at me and I gasped at the sight that greeted me. She had a small cut over her eyebrow and her right jaw was swollen.

"Some bitch jumped on me," she grumbled.

"Who?" I snapped. "I'll fuckin' kill 'er!"

I was surprised that I sounded like I could actually follow through with my threat.

I was not a fighter.

I mean I could stand up for myself when needed, but I wasn't exactly Mike Tyson.

I have been in one fight in my entire life, and that was only because my younger cousin Micah punched me in the face when we were kids to see if my blood was blue. She told everyone I was an alien from outer space with blue blood and the only way to prove I was a human was to punch me and make my nose bleed. I agreed because I didn't think it would hurt that much—I was wrong, very wrong, because it hurt like hell.

After Micah punched me and red blood streamed from my nose, we confirmed I was in fact human. I jumped on her then because I was in so much pain and decided that she needed to be punished for hurting me. Instead of dishing out a hiding, I received a black eye and a chipped tooth. Micah kicked my arse and it was the first and only fight I have ever been in. Regardless of my inability to bring the pain, if anyone hurt Aideen or Storm, I would go Bruce Lee on those fuckers.

That was a cold hard fact.

Aideen smiled at me and pulled me in for another tight hug. "I know you would, but I just want to go home now. Can I stay with you?"

Was that a serious question?

I shook her. "Of course, you bloody eejit."

Aideen laughed and so did the males who stood over us. I don't know how, but I forgot they were next to us. I quickly stood up and pulled Aideen with me. She wasn't exactly drunk, just a little tipsy. I didn't have to balance her or anything, but I still kept a tight hold on her just in case.

"This is Alec," Aideen said and lazily pointed to the man on the right who was openly looking me up and down, "and Kane." I tightened my hold on Aideen when I looked at Kane, the man on the left. He was just as tall and as muscular as the arsehole who was looking at my body, but he was scary looking. He had a large scar that curved around the left side of his mouth and some claw like scars going from his right temple and down through his eyebrow leaving gaps in the hairs like they were styled that way.

"Hi," I said lowly and avoided direct eye contact.

"Kane came to me rescue when Alec's girlfriend hit me," Aideen said and smiled at Kane, who smiled right back at her.

"She wasn't my lay for the night, not my girlfriend either... and I apologised for her actions," Alec said with a sigh.

I ignored Alec, the eejit who just spoke and looked at Kane when he smiled and felt myself instantly become relaxed. He didn't look scary when he smiled like that. I frowned though when the rest of what Aideen said settled in my brain. Before I knew it I let go of Aideen and shoved Alec in the chest as hard as I could. He wasn't expecting it so when I shoved him he lost his balance and fell back onto his arse with a grunt.

"That is for your bird hurtin' me friend and if I find out who the slut is I'm goin' fuckin' kill 'er!" I bellowed.

Aideen pulled me back by the arm and begged me to stop while Alec looked up at me with wide eyes before he looked to Kane, who stared down at him also with wide eyes and his mouth agape. A few seconds passed until they both burst out laughing like what just happened was the funniest thing ever. I saw red and tried to go for Alec

ALEC

again, but Aideen moved herself in front of me and pushed me back by the shoulders.

"I told you bro, she is a fucking hellcat!" Alec cackled as he gripped onto Kane's outstretched hand and was helped to his feet.

Kane continued to laugh as he shook his head. "I wish the twins had seen that, Dominic would have helped her hit you while Damien recorded it."

I had no idea what or whom they were talking about, but I pointed my finger dangerously over Aideen's shoulder at Alec and snarled at him.

"Keep laughin' pretty boy and I'll scratch up that face of yours!" I warned.

Alec stepped forward, a grin tugged at his mouth. "I'm finding myself highly attracted to you right now. Would you like to come home with me since you're already dressed for bed?"

I dropped my jaw in shock, and so did Aideen who spun around and shoved him in the chest, but didn't manage to knock him to the ground. "Knock it off! I appreciate you both helpin' me, but I won't have you treatin' me friend like she is one of your old clients, Alec. She is a good girl!"

Clients?

What the hell did *that* mean?

Alec grinned at Aideen before he flicked his eyes to me. "Oh, I'm bettin' there is a bad girl deep inside her somewhere. I'll just have to use my fingers, mouth, and cock to bring her out to play."

What. The. Fuck?

"Who the hell do you think you are?" I snapped.

He grinned and gave me a wink as he said, "Alec Slater, your next—or only—great fuck."

Was he for real?

"You're about to be Alec Slater—murder victim—if you don't shut that hole in your face!"

Kane cracked up with laughter as he reached for Aideen's arm and pulled her into him and away from me. "Please, don't interfere.

I've never seen a female, besides Bronagh, backtalk him like this before," he said to Aideen then brushed her blonde hair out of her eyes. The action caused her to melt into a puddle by the way she sagged into him.

I rolled my eyes at her then looked at Alec who had inched closer to me before I growled, "Try touchin' me, and you won't ever be able to have kids. I'm warnin' you."

Alec grinned and folded his arms across his board chest; it caused all his muscles that I could see to contract and tense. He settled on staying put, but openly raked his eyes over my body, mainly my legs, and it made me feel very uncomfortable.

"Stop lookin' at me you dirty bastard!" I growled.

Alec flicked his eyes up to me. "Why would you come outside dressed like *that* if you didn't want people to look at you?" he asked.

I clenched my hands into fists and took a step towards him. I had to tilt my head back a little bit because he was a lot taller than my five foot eight inches and when I realised that fact I felt intimidated, but I was not ready to back down.

"I came outside dressed in me nightdress because me friend needed me and gettin' dressed didn't cross me mind when you rang me, you bloody eejit."

He flashed his teeth at me when he smiled. "You sound like my bro's girl, she calls me an eejit a lot too."

I looked him up and down, my lip curled in disgust. "She must be kind 'cause there are a lot of words that would suit you much better. Batty boy would be two of them," I snarled then turned in Aideen's direction and found her kissing Kane. Not just smooching, she was completely necking with him. I walked forward, grabbed her arm and tugged her not so gently next to me.

When she was next to me I squeezed her arm and snarled, "Do you not remember the stranger danger film we watched when we were in school?"

Aideen gave me an are-you-serious look before she snickered and shook her head. "They aren't dangerous. Kane *saved* me from danger."

I pointed over my shoulder. "Yeah, and batty boy's *bird* put you in danger so let's go."

"I get the feeling that you're calling me gay," Alec said from behind me.

I set my jaw and continued to tug on Aideen as she frowned over my shoulder and said, "She is callin' you gay, but she doesn't mean it as an insult or anythin'. She's not homophobic, she just said it because she hoped it would piss you off."

Seriously?

"You aren't supposed to tell him that, Ado!" I snapped.

"Ado? I like that nickname," Kane's voice purred from my right.

He pronounced Ado so proper.

Ay-doh.

I pushed Aideen behind me, ignoring her complaints as I fixed Kane with a glare that wavered the longer I looked at him. "Listen, thanks for helpin' me friend after she got hurt, but she isn't goin' to thank you with some personal pole dancin' so give the flirtin' a rest."

Kane raised his eyebrows as he looked over my shoulder and asked Aideen, "You're a stripper?"

"No, I am a teacher," Aideen scoffed. "'No pole dancin' means no shaggin'."

Kane laughed then. "Your friend is banning you from having sex with me?"

"Yes," Aideen and I said in unison.

"And you're going along with it?" Alec asked Aideen as he rounded on us and leaned back against the same car Kane was leaning on.

They looked like a pair of fitness models and noticing that pissed me off.

"Yeah," Aideen sighed. "She is pretty big on no sex with strangers and... so am I."

Kane's eyes bore into Aideen and then he smiled as he said, "Pity."

"Uh huh," Aideen agreed with a sad sigh.

I rolled my eyes and said, "I'll stop off at the late night shop on the way home and buy you some batteries for your vibrator to get you through the night. You will be grand."

"Keela!" Aideen gasped and smacked my arse, it made me yelp and jump.

Both of the lads laughed at what I said and shook their heads as they continued to look at us. I got annoyed and said to Aideen, "Maybe they could apply to Perverts 'R Us, they fit the bill with those stares."

Aideen laughed and smacked my arse again.

"Excuse me?" Alec said.

Aideen was snickering as she said, "Keela's neighbour, Mr. Doyle, is a man who stares a lot so she named him Mr. Pervert and imagined him bein' the CEO of a company called Perverts 'R Us."

I narrowed my eyes when the two hyenas started laughing again —they seemed to do that a lot.

I angrily reached behind me and grabbed Aideen. "We're leavin'. I have to go home to Storm."

"Storm?" Alec questioned.

"Storm is her—"

"Boyfriend," I smiled as I cut Aideen off and gave her a go-along-with-me look. She looked back at me and I could see the amusement in her eyes as she nodded her head and looked back at Alec.

"Storm is pretty protective of her," she said.

Alex cocked an eyebrow. "If he is so protective then how come he let you come out here alone while dressed like that?"

He made it sound like my nightdress was skimpy!

I snarled and made a move forward to set him straight but Aideen put herself between Alec and myself before saying, "Storm is very hard to rouse durin' the night. He probably didn't even hear her leave, but he is still a great... lad."

I inwardly snorted.

"Yeah, and he will kick your arse for even suggestin' we have sex!" I stated.

Alec popped his head around Aideen and grinned at me. "I'm a lover, not a fighter."

Good news!

"You better back off then because one more crude comment and *I* will fuck you up, never mind Storm!" I snarled.

Alec bit down on his bottom lip and grinned at me, I knew he was thinking crude things so I glared at him which made Kane snort.

"Can we keep her? I like hearing someone put you in your place, the fact that she is a female is even better. You don't affect her bro, you're losing your touch." Kane chuckled and playfully shoved Alec when he settled back beside him on the car they were leaning on.

Alex continued to grin at me as he spoke to Kane, "It's still early, don't shoot me down so quickly, bro."

"I'll fuckin' shoot you," I murmured making Aideen snort as she reached for my hand.

"This has been... interestin'. However, Keela is right, we better get goin'."

"Thank you, Jesus," I cheered making Kane snicker before looking to Aideen.

He grinned at her and said, "I guess I'll see you around, Ado."

I narrowed my eyes at him. "I'm the only one allowed to call her Ado."

Kane flicked his eyes to me and smiled. "I like you."

I flushed but forced myself to stand up straight as I said, "Well, I don't like you or your pervy friend—"

"Brother. I'm his pervy *brother*," Alec cut me off making Aideen snicker.

I shoved her and glared at Alec before I looked back to Kane, who still looked at me with an amused expression. I cleared my throat and said, "I don't like you or your pervy *brother*. You're both clearly nothin' but trouble if the people you pal around with attack girls for no reason. You're both very fuckin' rude as well!"

I turned and grabbed Aideen's hand and took off walking away from the brothers and in the direction of my car.

"What? No goodbye kiss? *Now* who is being rude!" Alec's voice called out after us making Aideen cackle.

I grunted. "Fuck you!" I shouted without turning around.

"Name the time and place, kitten," Alec called back which caused Aideen to break out into a full on laugh.

Kitten?

I fumed in silence as I all but hauled Aideen across the dark car park and into my car. "Name the time and place, kitten," I mimicked Alec's voice which caused Aideen to laugh harder as she buckled her seat belt.

I buckled my own seat belt then started up my car. I pulled out of the space I was in and quickly drove out of the car park. I don't think I calmed down enough to breathe normally until we were on the Tallaght Bypass.

"Can you believe him? What a fuckin' dick!" I spat.

Aideen snorted. "I found that entire conversation hilarious."

I shook my head. "Well you shouldn't have. Look at your face, Aideen!"

Aideen sighed. "I know, but it honestly wasn't their fault. We were just havin' a good time when out of nowhere this girl jumped on me."

I gripped my steering wheel so tight that my knuckles turned white.

"Why were you even with them?" I spat.

I wasn't angry with her, I was just angry that she got hurt by some bitch.

"I wasn't even with them. Tonight was the first time I met them. I was out with Branna. Tonight was a small twenty-first birthday party for Bronagh. Branna, Ryder, Nico, and Bronagh just left. I was sat with Kane and Alec when a drunk girl came over and accused me of bein' Alec's latest shag. Alec laughed at the girl but didn't deny it so she jumped on me."

I grunted.

Branna Murphy was Aideen's friend and has been her friend since they were in preschool. Aideen is a few years older than me so she has known Branna longer than she has known me. I'm a grown woman, I'm not at all jealous of their friendship. Branna was cool after all. Her sister Bronagh was great as well, I was two years older than Bronagh, who turned twenty-one today. I had been invited to go out with everyone tonight, Aideen hounded me to go, but my body was beat, so I declined the invitation.

My thoughts calmed me down enough for me to loosen my white-knuckle grip on the steering wheel but I still shook with anger. "You should have let me punch 'em."

Aideen chuckled then lifted her hand to cradle her face. "You would have broken your hand! Did you see how big he was?"

I grunted and nodded my head. "His brother was even more muscular. Do they live at the gym or somethin'?"

Aideen snickered. "Branna said they have a gym in her house. 'Member I told you she moved in with Ryder and the oldest twin, Nico, moved in with her sister?"

I nodded my head.

"Branna didn't just move in with Ryder, she moved in with Alec and Kane as well. She said there is a gym room where the sittin' room should be and that they all work out a lot. You should see Nico; he's twenty-one and the lad is ripped. He is a fighter or somethin'."

I glanced at her wide-eyed. "Why the hell are you hangin' around walkin' tanks, Aideen?"

Aideen burst into a fit of giggles that made me grin even though I was mad.

"They are lovely—big and scary—but lovely."

I shivered when I pictured Kane's face, calling him lovely was not a word that I would use to describe him.

"How do you think Kane got those scars on his face? They are kind of severe."

Aideen sighed. "I've no idea what happened to him but he is still gorgeous!"

"You like his accent as well, right?" I questioned.

Aideen purred, "Oh my God. I could listen to him talk all day! He could make me wet by just sayin' 'Hello'!"

I rolled my eyes. "I swear you think with your dick."

Aideen cackled. "You mean vagina?"

"Yeah, I mean vagina but sayin' dick sounds better."

Aideen continued to laugh then hissed a little and covered her face with her hands. I glanced at her every so often during the five minute drive back to my apartment complex. I parked in my usual spot, then Aideen and myself got out of the car. After I locked it we quickly scurried across the car park and into my apartment building. We took the stairs two at a time until we got to the fifth floor where my apartment was located. I opened my hall door with lightening like speed because I didn't want to be caught by Mr. Pervert again dressed in just my nightdress.

Luckily, we got inside with no one seeing us. Aideen and I then went into the bathroom where I got out my first aid kit while she pulled her dress off then pulled down her underwear and sat on the toilet.

I was opening an antiseptic packet when I glanced up at her through the mirror and snorted, "Do you reckon lads do this?"

Aideen opened her eyes and lazily smiled at me as she said, "Willingly go to the toilet with another lad in the room? Nah, they would call each other gay."

I chuckled and looked back down to the first aid kit while Aideen finished up on the toilet. I turned when the toilet flushed and waited for her to wash her hands before I began cleaning her face up. She was four inches shorter than me now that her heels were off, so it made holding her head still a lot easier.

"Ow!" Aideen suddenly hollered which earned a bark from my bedroom.

"Go back asleep you fat shite!" Aideen shouted when I swiped the antiseptic wipe over a small cut above her eye.

I hissed at her, "Leave him alone, he isn't fat. He just has a thick coat!"

Aideen laughed through her hissing. "Yeah, a thick coat of blubber."

I gave her a firm look. "Don't slag me baby when I'm cleanin' you up. Me finger might slip and jam into your eye."

Aideen gave me a wary look and closed her mouth which made me inwardly grin as I finished cleaning up her face. When I was finished, she went into my bedroom to get some of my pyjamas to wear while I went into the kitchen to get a glass of water. I turned on the kitchen light then moved to the sink and filled up a glass and quickly gulped down the water. I looked to my left and noticed the envelope Mr. Pervert gave to me earlier, still unopened on my kitchen table.

"Storm, get off the bed... or at least move over!" Aideen's voice shouted from my bedroom.

I roughly rubbed the back of my neck and sighed. I glanced at the envelope once more before I shook my head and walked over to the kitchen light switch and flipped it off. I turned and walked towards the sounds of growling and shouting coming from my bedroom and decided that dealing with Storm and Aideen was enough to deal with for one night.

Whatever was in that envelope could wait until morning.

About the Author

L.A. Casey was born, raised and currently resides in Dublin, Ireland. She is a twenty-three year old stay at home mother to an almost two year old German Shepherd named Storm and of course, her five year old—going on thirty—beautiful little hellion/angel depending on the hour of the day.

She is the author of Amazon Bestselling book series, *Slater Brothers*.

CONNECT WITH ME

Facebook: www.facebook.com/LACaseyAuthor

Twitter: www.twitter.com/AuthorLACasey

Goodreads: www.goodreads.com/LACaseyAuthor

Website: www.lacaseyauthor.com

Email: l.a.casey@outlook.com

NOW AVAILABLE

FROZEN

DOMINIC (SLATER BROTHERS, #1)

BRONAGH (SLATER BROTHERS, #1.5)

ALEC (SLATER BROTHERS, #2)

COMING SOON

KANE (SLATER BROTHERS, #3)

AIDEEN (SLATER BROTHERS, #3.5)

RYDER (SLATER BROTHERS, #4)

BRANNA (SLATER BROTHERS, #4.5)

DAMIEN (SLATER BROTHERS, #5)

ALANNAH (SLATER BROTEHRS, #5.5)

BROTHERS (SLATER BROTHERS, #6)

Printed in Great Britain
by Amazon.co.uk, Ltd.,
Marston Gate.